THE OUTCAST'S BURDEN

THE OUTCAST'S BURDEN

Adam Daly

The ugly, awkward and urgent will have their day. Crawling out, skin and bone, from Ted Hughes' Slough of Despond, using a road map marked-up by Andrew Sinclair, Adam Daly delivers his millennial sermon. Spurned, hurt, maimed, this mental traveller slouches towards Hackney Marshes to be born. A non-fabulous fable, in antiquated clerical prose, that argues itself into a fugue of club-footed heroism. The miracle is that such material can self-generate in the days of spin and odourless slime. When no shit sticks, it is good to know that dirty protests can still leave their mark on the walls.

Iain Sinclair
Author, *London Orbital*

Browning wrote a poetic sequence called 'Madhouse Cells', and Adam Daly should certainly be found a cage adjoining Porphyria's Lover. *The Outcast's Burden* unfolds the conspiracy of a bunch of Luciferian oddballs, he aded by No Name Now, who collude in a plan to absorb humanity in the cause of all-devouring evil or some similarly carnivorous metaphysic.

The tale of the last gasp of humankind seethes with refuse rhetoric and detrital rhapsody. The nihilistic vitalism is well-sustained, as is the wit and audacious reach of metaphor – qualities that may ultimately grant *The Outcast's Burden* a place on the shelf next to *Frankenstein* or *Vathek* or, more fittingly, *Maldoror*.

Beneath the adolescent diabolism lurks a Miltonic grandeur and epic scope, in which the glory and terror of John Martin fuses with the mockery and disdain of Hogarth. Presumably the reader is supposed to applaud the drastic transformations of these malcontents – an all-encompassing unanimity admits no opposition to their nefarious master-plan. However, sheer Gothic effrontery wins through and, at close of play, we applaud the debut of a midnight visionary who, taking up the gauntlet thrown down by Bram Stoker and Lovecraft, has produced something of wider intellectual range and deeper satiric bite.

Paul Newman
Editor, *Abraxas*
Author, *A History of Terror*

Copyright © 2003 Adam Daly

Apart from any fair dealing for the purposes of research or private study, or criticism or review, as permitted under the Copyright, Designs and Patents Act 1988, this publication may only be reproduced, stored or transmitted, in any form or by any means, with the prior permission in writing of the publishers, or in the case of reprographic reproduction in accordance with the terms of licences issued by the Copyright Licensing Agency. Enquiries concerning reproduction outside those terms should be sent to the publishers.

Published by
Matador
12 Manor Walk, Coventry Road
Market Harborough
Leics LE16 9BP, UK
Tel: (+44) 1858 468828 / 469898
Email: books@troubador.co.uk
Web: www.troubador.co.uk/matador

ISBN 1 899293 33 7

Cover design and Map: E. R. Bartelt

All characters in this novel are fictional and bear no intentional resemblance to any actual person living or dead.

Typesetting: Troubador Publishing Ltd, Market Harborough, UK
Printed and bound by Cambrian Printers, Aberystwyth, Wales

Matador is an imprint of Troubador Publishing Ltd

Dedicated to the Defiant

The Writer is a cannibal – the Human Race his food
Obscurius

AUTHOR'S NOTE

My thanks are due to Jeremy Thompson at Matador for a fine production of this book, to Robert Bartelt for the inspired artwork and psycho-geographical map, and to Paul Newman and Iain Sinclair for their magnanimous commendations.

I should really allow the book to speak for itself, but would caution my putative Readers that it most certainly isn't some typical, neatly polished little literary confection, a pretty piece bien fait or nice, palatable offal of trendy fiction, still less an archly overknowing text stuck resolutely up its self-referential, pseudo-intellectual posterior, that they have in their hands here. The book is not a Novel at all, but is in many respects – fully in spite of its poetic conceits and philosophic aporias – what may be termed an 'Anti-Book', Anti-Literature, Anti-Postmodernism, Anti-just about everything else. In this capacity I like to think of it as an eructation of the Spirit – my own as much as the characters' themselves, if they can be called characters. And I know whereof I speak.

Adam Daly
December 2002

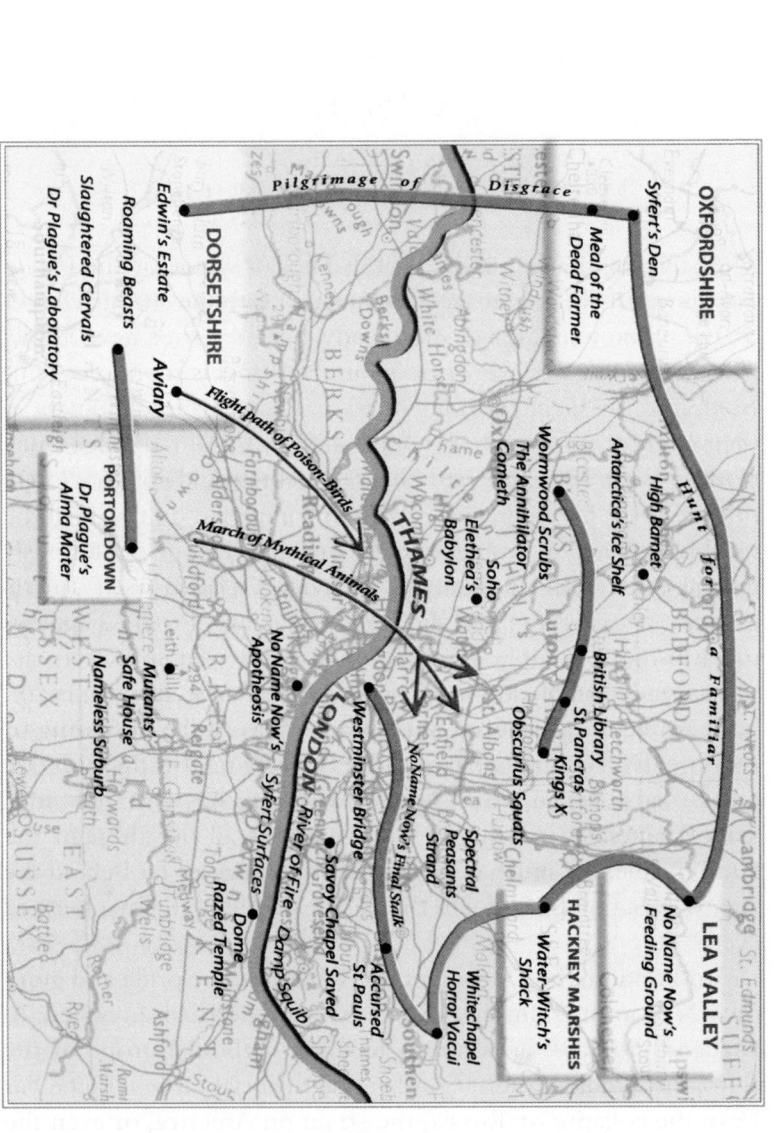

ONE

The Millennium is upon the World. The last whine of the *Fin-de-Siecle* is heard like a faint hush running beneath the chaotic chatter of the ubiquitous Media. All the advance-scenarios have finally been played out and every person on the Planet is soon to be confronted by the silent enormity of the greatest Historic Moment in their lives, or just another tick of the clock. All the mega-buck work-projects conceived and built to celebrate and commemorate this moment, have miraculously been completed on time. All the troubles still raging throughout the World have gone mysteriously into abeyance, as Humanity collectively prepares itself for its grandest partying leap into the Unknown – ever. Progress appears to have stopped – or rather, everything has slowed up as if a state of suspended animation had enveloped the Earth, allowing everybody to feel they have an equal part to play in the unfolding of Destiny. Everything appears to be converging, on the ultimate cross-roads. Yet in truth, little if anything has changed since Time Immemorial. The Human Mind has all but thought the Unthinkable, but much of Mankind still struggles far behind the Arrow-Head of Progress in flight. The World is still in a mess as ever.

In London, the Dome and the Wheel are the pride and glory of a Nation in triumphal mode. No-one here, or anywhere in England, thinks – or is meant to think – about Europe or the Euro, the Middle Eastern Conflict, the financial turmoil in the Far East, the collapse of Russia, the strain on America, or even the

Northern Ireland problem. Wars, Terrorism, nuclear and biochemical weapons, pollution, global warming, meteors, diseases, famine, drought, earthquakes, volcanoes, tidal waves, freak storms, economic crises, social breakdown, computer-chaos, corruption, crime, drugs, mental illness – to mention just a few of the World's worries – are not supposed to be on anyone's mind at present. Tony Blair is in his cool Heaven, and all is right with the Inclusive Society. The streets of the City are primed for a mass-address to the Almighty, and every living-room is a throbbing capsule of anticipation. Christianity and Capitalism are in a race to the finish, whilst traffic everywhere is drifting to a slow halt – vehicles and machines in a dream of reverence or a dream of dread.

Not everyone is accounted for in this build-up to an unparalleled event. There are some figures alone in the City, beyond the power of policing or caring, who have no family, friends, colleagues, fellow-exiles or anyone with whom to share the moment to come. To some, it may not mean very much – to others, it will scarcely even have dawned on them what the next nightfall will bring. They aren't awaiting their passage to a more privileged place. They are still as ever, surviving like dogs from one moment to the next. The calendar-clock is the relentless curse of their shrunken life-cycles. One of their number however, has been patiently preparing for this final day in the two-thousand year reign under the shadow of the Cross. He is resolved to make his mark, instead of slinking away in the dark corners of the City to shield himself from the Mysterium Tremendum and lick his ancient wounds. He knows he is the greatest one of his kind to have conceived a Plan of his own for the Millennium. He is so fused with his own intent, that on this day he is the only being of ultimate consequence on a God-deserted planet. For to-day is HIS day, and his deed of manifestation will crown and eclipse it in lieu of the figure of Christ in the Second Coming that will not come to pass. If Time has a future, it will not resemble its past.

No Name Now – the only 'name' he has chosen to attribute to himself – has awoken in a hidden pile of trash only he would choose to sleep in, and arisen like a fortified God of Garbage or

Lord-Leviathan of the lavatorial Underworld to stake his claim to the World beyond his long-possessed infernal patch. There is nothing of pathos about this figure. He has absorbed all the foreign bodies that other people's immune systems are unable to resist – he embodies the imperishable essence of the most toxic imaginable forms of degradation. He has been infinitely strengthened by that which would mortally weaken virtually any unarguable specimen of Homo Sapiens. On serious reflection, his antecedents would seem scarcely human in any event. Maybe only for the sake of some obscure or else trifling argument could he actually be described as human. He presents a solid spectre, affronting evolution. Moving with an uncanny alacrity belying his considerable bulk inside a rag-shell burden, he steps out of an unseen shadow into the sun-shaft of clear visibility – his face revealed to the passing species, which normally does not notice this shifting chimaera lurking with an unspeakable menace at the periphery of their senses.

In the sudden, soft-burning light, his appearance is world-repellently disgusting – one layer of grime for every Age of Man he has visited and abandoned. He clearly inhabits his own stench like the rarest of solitary predators, secure at last from besiegement and extinction. Hirsute and hairless by turns in the past, he has shaved his head so often it has since sprouted beards. His face – while without distinguishing marks as such – has the look and air of a desecrated Icon, restored to a mask, ground to a cypher, enduring as live rubble. His eyes display the emptied allure of multiple monstrosities poised to strike – for an infinity, if need be. His body is racked and ravaged, yet possessed of supernaturally sinuous sources of strength, endowing it with all its recoveries from unendingly exacting pains. He carries his world with him from place to place, like an upright tortoise of savage disposition, the numberless pockets of his shell-coat filled with the detritus of starved appetites and deranged pursuits, from chewed conkers to mouldy scripts. The dried sodden excrescences of once-worn shoes have grown into his feet like huge, leathery, fungoid corns. His hands extend from the matted grey skin of his clothing like taloned crabs soaked in sulphur. There is no organic divide between the microbial denizens of his host-body and the craving parasites of its rotted shroud. He is Diderot's devil, risen from the black pools of dessicated life-forms.

He resolutely and rhythmically stalks his passage from the old Artillery Ground in Whitechapel – a preserved warren of alleys where faceless figures in black cloaks once vanished into swirling white mists only to reappear in the Grimoires of the Gothic Imagination – in the clear direction of the once-walled, neighbouring city of suited aliens, with its glistening towers of High Finance threatening to topple over onto the hovel-wastes of a lost territory cringing far beneath them. In his previous Satanic spells the City was cast into a rubble-plain of twisted glass and metal outcrop, a surreal landscape of Daliesque debris, through which only the dispossessed survivors of his psychic bomb-blast would wander and clamber at their demoniacal leisure. The Real IRA could never have begun to imagine such a scenario within the narrowed focus of their purely political pathology. But today, he would simply traverse the length of the gross, centripetally pulling, Roman legacy, on route to a more specially divined site lying some distance beyond, to precipitate his slow-nurtured, deep-flamed, Protean heresy. His eyes do not move from the animus of their fixity – knowing as he does like the marks on his epiphenomenal claws, the stone-map of urban depravity separating him from his destination – as his bestial physiognomy draws, rather than drags, itself towards somewhere other than Bethlehem, to be something other than born. Other eyes he ignores or negates – blind to human curiosity, immune to human offense. He claims the souls of wide berthing passers-by like Grendel on the astral, ingesting then discarding them in films of dried ectoplasm, bequeathing an intangible wake of unknowing dislodgement. Anybody rousing an antenna beneath the threshold of his visual ken, is in mortal spiritual danger. No radius is safe within the Circle of the Anti-Christ – his scent alone rings this great city of pestilence.

The square mile itself is operationally dead on this day of all days. Odd people saunter or else hurry through the rifts along the valley-floor of this architectural mountain-range, this deserted aerodrome filled with forests of obelisks. A powerful sense of the End of History pervades the place and the being of those in it, if only in transit to elsewhere. Mammon's blocks play a dark duet with Wren's spires, crowned by the light of St. Paul's. But a shadow of cancerous cloud falls across the Sun as No Name Now draws near to the risen Phoenix of the Great Fire, the tricentennial monument to Rational Religion. He cannot pay the tithe to enter – and would not, in any event – possessing no money, in requiring none. So he curses the Cathedral with a shower of poisoned rain *en passant*. People scatter towards the nearest shelters, leaving him to plot his macabre Pilgrimage without obstruction, bearing the true unlicensed freedom of the perennial ghost-city. He does not look up, or shift for a moment from his line of sight, as the high facade of the Cathedral looms above him on his prophetic descent to the old Roman Strip.

Morning has passed into afternoon, and the winter-dusk will soon envelop London like a fall of Vesuvian soot – a black miracle of Astronomy eclipsing the Heavens for immeasurable aeons. The planned fireworks display over the Thames around Midnight will go out like a star-map in a sudden power-cut – squibs of sentiment returning to a sardonic soil. The ecstatic revelries of millions of Millennial seers will be turned in seconds on the faltering chimes of Big Ben into the chaotic wails of a nightmare panic, rumbling and rushing through the very Geology of the Metropolis and beyond. No Name Now sees this Vision already in the actual Sphere of his extended influence – it CANNOT NOT happen! He KNOWS it will be his prize for outdoing Sisyphus in the long trials of Fate. For many years he has mined HIS boulder with the ingredients of Cataclysm and Collapse – and soon the wretched hill will no longer exist, and the Gods will be blasted and sucked into interminable oblivion! Bedlam beckoned to him once in some other, long-forgotten incarnation. But no institution on Earth could reach him now or pull him into its protectionistic clutches – whether for the safety of mankind or his own rehabilitation. He is so far beyond the pale of human social membership, his merest existence is a matter of the most terrible conjecture – only ever to be confronted when he made his presence catastrophically felt. And this he is just on the verge of doing, not purely for the sake of vengeance – though Satan knows he has cause enough for that – but above all else for the sake of a starker scheme of things, not a higher or even a truer, but a sheerly STARKER scheme in its very essence; for everything not of its essence could not endure beyond this Day to end all Days. The most ruthless simplification of planetary civilization is imminent, and the 'terrible beauty' resulting from it will truly dwarf anything ever envisioned in the poetic imagination of a William Butler Yeats.

As he nears Charing Cross, he conjures revenants from the Peasant's Revolt of 1381 foreshadowing the recent Poll Tax Riots – blessing the incendiary angels of the old Savoy Palace whose spirit-tissue leavens the ages of the local air in pyramidal echelons of inviolate flame. No Name Now sees the flames, smells them, hears them, feels their roaring intensity as he moves through the charcoal residues of all their futures. The long-feuding spirit of England is nowhere better captured than in this still surviving space of invasion and uprising, the blood-spattered grave of London's torn and divided heart. 'We will not be ruled,' he says to himself in the gathered voice of every unnamed, downtrodden and fallen hero in the one great War never mentioned in the History Books: the War against all arbitrary Power and Authority, all Established Hierarchy. 'Self-Rule is the only Rule. I am gifted to deliver this liberty unto every wretch who has suffered its denial in his span of Life. We will dive through the high wave and black curtain of Destiny, leaving our tyrants drowning and damned in its crashing descent. I am risen among them, not sent, to help spawn new cultures from the ingested compost of universal despair.'

Frissons of current escape from him into the surrounding air, suddenly whirling down into a sump of infestation foaming out into the space that will forever outlast John Nash and his dull dutiful gentrification of a dangerous terrain – the space BEFORE Trafalgar Square, the small wilderness bordering the toxic gems of

St. Giles. Its present stained munificence makes no impression as he heads for the ignominious parade of Whitehall – a street of taverns and tenements before Gilbert Scott et al got their gilded Neo-Gothic hands on the still essentially enduring grubbiness of a thoroughfare echoing the fall of a burning Tudor Palace. He throws up a cascade of treacherous phlegm over General Haig's equestrian statue, a gestated tribute paid by millions of dead youths calcifying beneath the green and red tomb-lids of resurrected French fields. The Ministries of State suddenly seem VULNERABLE in his eyes – so close to hand and unguarded in the space between, even unoccupied at a swift, expropriating glance – as to present on this Day of all Days an unparalleled opportunity for a risen power of the elemental earth to overrun and stamp them into extinction. He feels there is no need to stir up a mob – though the Populace deserves to have ITS Day too – as he alone could steal through the chambers of corruption caging him out, like an astral dragon consuming all the secret histories of the Nation-State in a single raging fire of etherial breath. No Police-Force in the Land could stop him.

But to make such a gesture at this hour – in the late summer of the diurnal cycle – would serve only as a premature distraction from his midnight-coup, stealing his own thunder from the soon gathering clouds heralding terminal winter on the Millennial cusp. The concentration of his curse in the next nine hours must not be diluted at all in any frivolous, wasteful expenditure of his hideous accumulation of talents. The Cabinet-Office had already been stormed by Anarchists on one occasion, during the dull calm of the mid-Victorian era – before the Crimean War, when other potential insurgents were dragooned into service and conveniently killed off in the time-honoured manner of regimes soaking up dissent. The plot had failed of course, like the Cato and Sidney St. conspiracies before and after it. The ring-leaders were executed, and Cabinet-meetings were held in secret at No. 10, Downing St. To No Name Now, the bomb-throwing antics of such antediluvian agitators were akin to the unruly splashes of infants on first discovering the delights of displaceable bath-water. These infants, and many others besides, had all since grown – and become HIM.

He registered the Cenotaph as he passed – walking up the middle of Whitehall like a maggot-eating Magus of the Art of the Invisible, quelling the uncomprehending stares of drivers as he had pedestrians before – with neither reverence nor contempt, nor indifference, but with a sublimely strange and silent resolve. The epicentre of Power lay just ahead of him, as false a Meridian-point in his counter-cosmogeny as Greenwich and that shiny bronze marker behind Le Seueur's statue of Charles I that had evaporated in his eyes without his proffering so much as a solitary spit. Like Wordsworth before him, he was making for Westminster Bridge. Unlike Wordsworth, he would arrive at dusk to behold little of true grandeur – biding his time not for a Poem but for an End to end all Ends, the jet crown of all Apocalypses.

TWO

In Anno Domini – Anno Diaboli – 1967, a curious incident took place. An abandoned infant was discovered in the Hackney marshes by a woman who had been living in a self-built shack in the region for years, left to her own mad but essentially harmless devices by the Police and Local Authority. To the local population she was known as the 'Water-Witch', their curiosity tempered by fear. Children walking or playing in the area were warned by their parents not to go near her, as she would often appear in her tousled rags, black hair blowing in the wind revealing a swarthy, alien face, and shout angrily at people in a language no-one comprehended – a language of the stars, it sounded to some. Though she never moved within actual striking range of anyone, and seemed content merely to voice her anger in a ritual fashion for a few minutes before retreating inside her abode. It was a mystery how she managed to provide for herself in this fetid environment, for she clearly had no money, no family, no friends, and no work or welfare – yet she was miraculously self-sufficient in her little space of barren isolation. If she was wretched when she first appeared in this district as if from nowhere, then she was no more wretched ten years later on – albeit no less wretched either. The constancy in her wretchedness bespoke some innate capacity to nourish herself, belied by the apparent absence of all nutrients in her surroundings. Local rumours abounded that she had some fortune stashed away, or else stole by night – a broomstick burglar! But nobody without authority had dared to investigate, and nobody with authority had seen fit to. And so she had become and remained, an unassailable, though unassimilable part of the furniture on the borderland of local lives.

The infant was wrapped in stained, light-coloured cloth when she stumbled across it at dawn one morning, placed in undergrowth near the bank of the canal that ran behind her shack across the fields that extended flatly toward the camping-site at their boundary – a city of barbarians perilously close to her tiny, unfenced kingdom. She often kept a strange vigil through the starlight hours as she stalked in ceremonial circles about the centre of her stranded universe, in keeping with a magic radius known only to her and bound by the minutest of peripheral points – blades of grass, for example. So her acute vicinity-vision enabled her not to overlook the comparatively unsuspicious package, which on inspection was to reveal the most shocking surprise of her meagre, if equally mysterious existence. In the deranged exigency of her condition, there was a sufficient vestige of maternal frustration for the spectacle of the unclothed baby to awaken an instinct of curiosity and care. What struck her first, and most of all in her warped lucidity, was the sheer SILENCE of the creature. And though it was far from clean or showing any signs of having been initially well cared for, it still looked defiantly strong and healthy. Its complete lack of hair did not impinge on her at all, drawn as she was by the reflective oddity of its eyes. She breathed a few half-formed words of insane intimacy, blew on its face softly then hurriedly lifted it up while still in its wrapping, cradling it briefly in her rags like a marooned Madonna before spiriting herself and her new cargo across the fields to her home – where once inside, she shut the door firmly behind her on the unknowing, unwanted world outside.

From that moment onwards she resolved, and contrived, to be the infant's mother – without the world being aware of the fact. And it so transpired that no news of the missing baby came to light – the world never even knew of its existence, let alone its disappearance. In her own manner of understanding, the infant had been left for her by its mother, who did not want it or could not care for it. It was a gift from an absent god, and beyond this she felt quite unconcerned about its antecedents and the possible consequences of her act of spontaneous theft. The first thing she did on the day of her discovery was to dig furiously, with her hands, to create a chamber beneath the caked floor of her dwelling – a dark, soil-encased manger – with enough space for her charge to rest, feed and grow in a coven of Satanic serenity. It took her all day to achieve this, leaving room for herself to crawl through from above and snuggle up to her find, illuminated in his swaddling-clothes and his cot of earth by one of many oil-lamps she had found while foraging in skips and waste lots. The piles of soil she packed into bags, then heaved by night to the canal where she dumped them. The entrance to her little child-coven she could always cover over with a rug or mat, so her grave subterranean secret should be well sealed and protected from any hypothetical scrutiny. The only thing remaining to be done was to provide nourishment, and this she knew how to do – presuming an instant kinship in the realm of animalized appetites.

In the eyes of a God of the impossible viewpoint, the uncommunicated, if not incommunicable truth of her predicament contained the alarming fact that in her innumerable years of privation she had grown capable of consuming ABSOLUTELY ANYTHING. Nothing was so degraded that it did not offer some small measure of nutrition at least to a body and constitution so long inured to toxicity as to positively thrive on it – to suffer cold turkey in its absence. And as her breasts were now dessicated fonts of dried and rancid milk, there was nothing else to be done but to begin building the infant's immunity to a diet that no normal human mother would contemplate even after a month of starvation in a vast, deserted landscape. There was a shortage of drinking-wells in the district, and in years past she would walk a long distance to the nearest public convenience to collect water in large plastic cartons. If the washroom basin-taps weren't working – as was often the case – she would place the cartons in a lavatory-bowl and then flush water into them until they were full. She did this so she could avoid going to public houses, where the stares of drunken, lecherous men enraged her to the point where blue-dressed guardians would have to be called for. Then one day she returned to her shack to discover that it had been broken into, and although nothing had been stolen – nothing there could have been wanted by any mere thief – her few surviving earthly possessions had been rummaged and scattered about. From that day, she decided she could not risk moving beyond a given radius of her abode. And so began her obsession with keeping circular vigils, day and night. Also some means had to be found of living off marsh-nutrients. It rained the day after and she left more cartons out to collect the drops. But she soon tired of this and took to sucking the water from the surrounding grass, which sated her thirst after a few minutes. However, this was not going to be a viable option during a long hot summer. So the next day she went to the nearby canal, where she forced herself to overcome her revulsion at sampling the water. The dank, microbial soup descended inside her – a thick, brown bile in contra flow – to land like glutinous turds of mercury in the pit of her stomach; whereupon she waited for symptoms to start shooting through her. But strangely, no symptoms ensued – apart from a mildly clinging sensation of nausea, which didn't strike her as deviating greatly from her habitual range of toxic sensations. From that day on the canal served as her personal reservoir, her free trough.

In the case of food, much the same development had occurred. She could no more walk long distances to collect discarded fruit and vegetables, or even fish and meat – on the ground at street-markets by day and behind supermarkets by night – so had steeled herself to consume grass, weeds, moss, lichen, slime, berries, fungi, leaves, horse-chestnuts, wood-bark, etc. Her resistance to toxins had passed through more thresholds than had the most ravenous hyena or skunk. Her body-chemistry had changed to the extent that her human classification grew problematic. Her inods were a mush of metamorphic organisms self-sustained within the pasty shell of her skin. Maybe at some stage in this process of cellular transformation the organisms could nourish her through their own regeneration, and she had grown so accustomed to the diet of an animal that she remained wholly addicted to it thereafter. And it seemed natural to her when she had another being to nurture, to feed it just as she fed herself. And this she proceeded to do, slowly fattening up her little feral foetus with the uncultivated produce of infested nature – procuring him as a homunculus of unwholesomeness. Week after week, month after month, year after year passed, and at no point did her unregistered possession see the light of day. But he grew, nourished as he was by the soily ingredients of her daily provisions, curiously never succumbing to illness other than the illness of being alive in a naturally contaminated condition to which he adapted himself like an internalized chameleon alighting on a secreting culture of bacterial mould.

She had to enlarge his coffin-like cot in stages to accommodate his stretching responses to growing-pains, his urge to kick out and clutch, to crawl, and finally to stand and walk. He emitted unconfigurable sounds, gestating some idiom of his own – close to hers, yet strangely separate. Eventually she permitted him to ascend from his earthen cave and then orient himself in the universe of her room-chamber. She educated him after a fashion, in the geography of her world – their world – its furniture and utensils, its bounded space filled with almost unbounded diversion. There were no books, but she vaguely and obscurely knew of their existence, sensing the as yet undefined hunger in him for their future edification in an unnoticed realm beyond the aluminium-shuttered crucible of his protected emergence. In the meantime, the world was a kind of book waiting to be read and then burned. Her minute world of sedimental slime and arcane junk sat like a jet coal at the centre of the vast world extending around and beyond, without end and dead to her comprehension. THINGS were her texts, in the Alexandrian Library of her effluent den. She read them with her eyes and hands like a robber of signifiers, a scholar of shit – this last proving a great insulator against cold, and fertilizer of exotic weeds from the stool-beds carpeting the walls and floor. The cross-fertilization of hers and her protegee's excreta symbolized a potent inversion of the suckling symbiosis of Madonna and child – a faecal spawning of the Great Whore's phantom-offspring – save this puritan pairing of impure isolates branded the brothels of Babylon as surely as the Church of Christ with the burning black crucifix of an impenetrable Heresy born of elements ever unredeemed.

Things of no use to a mortal human piled up in their own spaces like a fungal scrapyard – broken bits of bedding, torn papers, rusted items of cutlery, shredded clothing, discarded shells, match-boxes, pen-knives, coins, bags, dead flowers, tobacco leaves, peeled tin plates, cracked cups, encrusted mugs, charcoal-covered pots and pans, cheesy boots – solid slag-heap fixtures, defining the Figure of the room. No cooking or washing could conceivably have been done there – nothing remotely domestic or practical. Her detrital collections were the grounded baggage of her former vagrancy, as indecipherably necessary to her continued existence as the sea-sick symmetries of her chutneyed inods. Each possession was her child – a buried Talisman at the threshold of breath. The living, breathing entity that moved with adolescent agility and stealth, threatening to grow through the roof of its confinement, shared in the legacy of her skin cumulus as the latest child-thing/thing-child as yet unweaned off her spirit presence. It was no more curious about her origins than she was about its – home was hell, hell was home. Nothing else was normal, no question arose. The answer was to continue growing, consuming, questing. Her door would one day open onto the world it could claim, like a minotaur released after years of nurturing in the night of a lost life to crush and devour the denizens of an inhospitable planet. It was always evolving a will of its own, from something that took precedent even over the clinging will of its guardian.

Then one day she decided to let it – him – out, although only after nightfall during a warm, summer spell, when children had gone home and adults feared to venture abroad. The odd adolescent gang stalked the marshes after dusk, but she'd risk such an encounter tonight for the sake of exposing her treasure to the bestowal of the stars. He drew a strength from the elements as he grasped the space around him, swallowing the air like a fortifying, fresh poison and pushing his legs out past the walled boundaries of his only exercise-yard. He was struck by the sudden, new, visual expanse as by a spectacle sprung at him from the bleakest swamps of phantasmagoria. The grass seemed to spread like a carpet of calthrops, shockingly soft underfoot. The dimly bright darkness awakened in him the first stirrings of alertness to the reach of Space and its variety of configuration. The muted sound of distant traffic struck him with all the rumbling force of an alien visitation, shocking him into a fuller awareness of some OTHER Species' encroachment. Hackney's High Rise Towers flickered like a fleet of landed spacecraft – panoptic beacons in the suburban swamp. They drew his eyes into them like conical daggers penetrating the cracked and peeling skin of Civilization. Encountering no other earthling within their orbit, the omniverous couple stalked the Hermetically plotted parameters of their grass-kingdom till weariness wended them homeward and hellward.

From then on the Anti-Christ without antecedents thrived on these nightwalks like an organism spawned in an oceanic cave, starved of photosynthesis while feeding on the live nutrients of pitch-dark colonies. The daylight was a glimpsed rumour of contrast during sleeping cycles. Finally he became blind to it, conquering with the radiation of rot. He felt himself fully prepared to depart for danger, to hide in the shade of a false heaven and there to educate himself to the enormity of his burgeoning mission, his abysmal vocation. But first he must escape his Protector, who he still could not name in a language recognizable to Man. Yet some strangulated sound emitted from his lips might have transliterated into the English word 'MOTHER', even if their bond was biological only in the roots of soil and slime and the elemental attachments of the sterile estranged. Deliberating in his own silent tongue on the need to dissolve this bond and circulate among the cells of gathering cosmic cancers shadowing the healthy body of Humankind, he eventually resolved on a course of action. He would EAT his mother, then abandon their home to mundane puzzlement – spiriting himself away into the little and great wildernesses of the nameless landscape extending beyond his immediate ken into the maw of his larger Identity. She had fed him without limit, so she would become his food. He now possessed a strength engendered in the extremest ferocity of Supernature, the raw fire of sinewy beasts, the exploding tear of clawed deformities. None of this she suspected, seeing in her charge the innate docility of helpless foundlings. Her sources of strength were vocal and spirited, but his were instinctual and alien – concealed like hard stones in malleable rags.

He would kill and eat anything – or body – that interposed itself between him and his goal of enveloping the earth with the breath and matter of that all-destroying demon living inside him and propelling his destiny, like the greatest ordainer of written and unwritten curses. He would discover spaces in which to nurture his powers beyond scrutiny, before choosing the day – and this day was already in a sense chosen for him without his foreknowledge even – on which to announce himself to the world in his truest colours, abandoning disguise whereupon the wings of the most treacherous raptor would spread in triumph across Space itself. He could live in confinement only while growing – once grown, he must claim, conquer and consume all before him. This obscure blueprint of his evil being communicated itself in signs before Babel, seeding messages in the formation of tongues. And so it was soon after, that he ripped out the throat of his begetter without birth as she sang her sweet diatribe of the poisoned earth – to jar no more on the ears of her soulless, freak-starred son. When he had fed to extinction on the bloodied remains of the woman, leaving no trace of her deviant DNA in the faecal time-capsule of her entombed existence, he abandoned the shack the same night and vanished into the heretical hinterlands of an ancient domain the spirit of which he would soon infuse with his breath.

THREE

The mystery of the missing woman, her home quite intact, only came to light after several weeks, when some intrepid youths – missing her shouting performances, with the opportunities she gave them to bait her further – braved her threshold to find the shack entirely empty. The stench inside was so violently obnoxious, it precipitated them into a terrified run all the way back to their respective homes. Word spread through the neighbourhood till eventually the Police were informed and they decided to investigate. Wearing protective masks to shield themselves from any toxic effects of the clinging odour, they patiently exhumed every item of junk and spot of filth left in place, finding nothing at all to indicate her whereabouts, her intentions or whether she was alive or dead. But before they concluded their search, one officer managed to unstick the infested, crawling rug that had covered the entrance to the little underground chamber, prompting a collective estuarian murmur of 'Eureka'. And although no human remains were to be found there, the discovery of the rotten shreds of swaddling-clothes in which the water-witch's monster-child was first found and then laid to living rest in its earthen cradle, occasioned a sudden rush of frenzied forensic speculation. She must have abducted an infant and disappeared with it somewhere – or murdered it perhaps?! But there had been no report of any missing infant in the district for some time, and there were no unsolved cases remaining on local Police-files. Perhaps she had had a child all along and had somehow managed to conceal its existence from the neighbourhood? If this were the case, then it was of some urgency that both of them should be found. Even outcasts laid a claim on the attentions of the great legal machine.

And so a search was organized – for a non-existent dead woman and an uncognizably evolved child – while a forensic team analyzed the remains of the swaddling-clothes, establishing that they could not have been worn for between fifteen and twenty years. So it was not a child that was being sought, but an adolescent or young adult instead. The tenor of the investigation then shifted subtly, it now being considered that the roles of abuctor and abductee, or worse, could have been the reverse of what had initially been assumed. But whilst the Police had an image of the woman in their memory, which an artist was able to represent on paper – the resulting photograph stunning the General Public into a state of nameless horror, of silence before the Alien – they of course had no image whatever of the other presumed player in the mystery-drama they were pledged to fathom and resolve. The suggestion that the woman might have obtained the swaddling-clothes for an imaginary infant, or even worn them herself, was swiftly dismissed when evidence of two distinct 'bodies' of excreta lining the walls of the shack was confirmed in laboratory tests. This was the only real forensic evidence available to prove that two people had been occupying the shack for some given period of time. The public response to Police appeals was perhaps inevitably somewhat muted. Nobody had seen the mysterious woman for weeks or months even, and they had absolutely not the remotest inkling of her still more mysterious abductor, if that was what he was, or if he really existed. It seemed to some as if they were being implored to keep an eye out for the Devil himself, whose innumerable guises offered no clue as to his true identity. And the Devil of course – or the Devil in question – may have been female. Forensic evidence alone couldn't resolve this conundrum.

While the local community was perplexed by the case, the nation as a whole can hardly be said to have been in a state of panic. Disappearance was an occasional fact of life, and until a body was found there was no compelling evidence that a killer was at large, never mind a serial one. The alarm over the matter arose more from the sheer strangeness of the missing woman herself than from a worst case scenario portending what had befallen her. Maybe she had simply decided to take herself off one night, with or without her putative child/companion, to some other part of London or England. Even outcasts had this right – indeed, especially outcasts, who were never welcome anywhere. And it was above all else the prospect of being confronted by her and having to become involved in her case by reporting her sighting to the Police that made people uncomfortable most of all. The black magic inexorably if unintentionally captured and conveyed in the artist's profile was confined to this curse alone – so far. It concentrated its power in the very precipitation of the drawn face as a figure to be studied – holding intact the correspondences between source and facsimile, the accidents straying from design. This power got carried over to invoke its own mystique. The drawing didn't require to be technically good, or to represent evil in a deliberate, conscious manner. It could not but do other than conjure an essence that struck its own reflection in the eye of its own expression. Viewers caught its contagion on the rebound from their own looks.

FOUR

The escaping, predatory grotesque looked so inhumanly hideous as to warrant a national alert if seen, quite irrespective of whether he was linked in the mind of a witness with the missing woman. No tramp looked so terrible that a man might mistake him or her for a satyr-like beast, though some came to resemble humungus-like creatures or saprophytes grown from discarded piles of refuse or rotting vegetation. But under the clinging, curdling excrescences of slime-baked rag-cloth and baggage, enough signs of fleshy physiognomies still survived and protruded to argue their antecedence as members of the human species. However, this creature was different. It appeared as though it were merely mimicking human form, with odd deviations substantiating its air of supernal monstrosity. It was wired up by ravenous demons, obeying unknown laws. The gleam in its red, charcoaled eyes segued through unseen spaces into the spring of its step, the star-shoot of its claws. The blackest hair cascaded in animal profusion from its scalp, and body too. Though the latter was so mummified in a patchwork quilt of cotton and fur, filched and assembled from dossers' cast-offs over unchronicled stretches of time – an archeological map of eroding fibre, a maypole-tree of decayed confetti, a scarecrow of Supernature – that the hair was only visible on the head. The consumed remains of the Water-Witch's similar coat of contamination had combined with the organic sewage of compounds seeping through the skin into the fabric of Evolution's Mask. The whole apparition, as yet unseen by Humankind, coursed over the Hackney marshes beneath the Sickertian sickle of a moon shining faintly through a carpet of brown night in the unknowing direction of the Lea Valley.

The creature – call it what you will – came to rest in a thick clump of tree bushes near to one of the long meandering paths that cross the many miles of conserved country twisting like a Thuggee's dagger through the ringing vastnesses of East London. This terrain would be its home for the unforeseen future, providing it with the alternating shelters and spaces that it needed to rest and wander by day and night respectively. When the first dawn of its migration rose, it struck it not in the eyes but got drunk in with the dark. The day was obliterated in a colourless carnage. With the stealth of a Golem Predator it gripped the geography of its new domain, educating its intelligence to a strategy of survival. The river it could drink and be immersed in, the mud-banks and foliage concealed its food. The trees and bushes were spy-holes affording views into the weak flesh and awaiting viscera of the passing featherless bipeds rejected by Diogenes, who had tossed a skinned chicken over a rival's garden-wall! When the early morning dog-walkers ventured across the Lea Valley, sensing no watching presence in their midst or anything different from any other day, the cannibal-vigilant noted their features from behind green cover – the soft skulls like gulls' heads, the unenergized gaits and bred faces – and bided his appetites. At the same time long lines of Police were patrolling the Hackney marshes, combing every ditch, copse and hidden space for a sign of the Water-Witch. As yet no similar operation had been mounted for the Lea Valley. In time the monster lurking in its outcrops would sense danger over limitless distance, deciphering the remote signature of uniformed Guard. His antennae would thrust through blankness, like Language.

Days and nights passed, the Police-searches proving fruitless as their unsubstantiated quarry grew into his acquired territory like a winged yeti, an avatar of invisibility, sticky fanged and webbed, the nigredo of this no-man's land. Then it sprang an impulse to clutch and consume – carrying a woman away in an interval of blurred vision to pound her flesh, crack her bones and crush her inods; gulping the squashed remains as would a wild cat a pile of chopped meat left in a backyard. The trail of terror was now begun – to wrap itself like a girdle of gore around the globe, by degrees choking the breath of Humanity from the lungs of Nature. From Waltham Abbey to the Thames, and then out into the seas and other lands of the world the compost of excreted bodies would circulate in discrete, diabolical currents and fructify in beds of biodegradation. Some specimens he would spare, gracing suitable males of the species into the gang of the Beast with spirit-showers and stigma-spores, while inseminating the female counterparts with gene-freak deformities evading termination at birth. These would bear the Outcast's Burden through the Millennial twilight and out beyond the radius of all Religion into the enigma of the Unnameable. But the exorcist armies – if allowed near enough for inspection – would search scalp, armpits, genitalia, orifices and scabbed skin in vain for a revealing glimpse of Satan's superlative cricket-score. The flipped serpent of the Double Helix had no need of a number to fulfil its undecoded destiny.

The Book of Revelations had no remote bearing on the emergence of this ominous ogre – being, well, a book, and nothing more. St. John was no more prescient than that old fraud Nostradamus in the matter of prophesy, enshrining his wet dreams in the thebaid of a guaranteed future best-seller of dubious provenance! There was no SECRET in Evil, it just manifested occasionally – as did Genius and madness. Only the lottery of luck – or the machinery of manipulation – threw up polar opposites consumed with vengeance to an Olympian degree, a nature-warp eating the heart out of careless Life in periods that seemed cyclical on inspection, but corresponded to cosmic cataclysmic forces never predicated on the Clock, the Calendar and the Chronicle. The Great Beast of the Lea Valley was akin – in nature and evolved appearance – to an abortifacient of the Human Species, its mother's eyes swiftly shielded from it before being discarded without official register. Its infantile resilience had been a rogue feature of its innate freakishness, enabling it to grow into its grotesqueness with the aid of its feral, nocturnal nurturing. He who hath Intelligence may interpret it without a number – or a name – but instead as a thing of the night or effluent of a dark star. If Romulus and Remus built Rome in rather longer than a day, No Name Now – as it would soon come to signify itself in the wake of a language – would destroy it in rather less than a day of sidereal duration by his reckoning, being an infernal incubus of infinitely greater powers than any mere wolf-man. Rome of course would come to serve as a still apt metaphor for the general condition of Modern Civilization, at least in its late Imperial throes of auto-destructive barbarity in the grip of Christian contagion, when he mastered the practice of reading human texts in quiet corners of public libraries, disguised as a tramp in a later incarnation before death.

Armageddon and Apocalypse were only metaphors for a state of convulsion, the blood-tide of human affairs drawing to a temporary, if transforming close. The Whore of Babylon was likewise a metaphor for all women spawning deviant specimens and the scum of the Species, a necessary act of Lethean labour and gargoyle gestation consequent on harbouring the sperm-seas of the promiscuous princes of darkness. Frankenstein killed his creator, and so the Beast ate his mother to ravage and impregnate the many whores of contemporary Babylon. His origin was not in electricity but a Caesarian continuum. No Name Now's food of the future would be a string of women/whores and men/masses stretching out as long as the Lea. John Williams and Jack the Ripper had nothing on him already, though the Malthusian Magus in the making would later sup on the cadres of Macchiavelli's Legatees in preference to the shrivelled fat of the hoi polloi, being then the Supreme Anarch of the atomized soul. He would even befriend a few of the most driven out members of the Race he otherwise preyed on – the profanest ex-communicants of all – to savour a near-echo and to induct them into the extremest Ars Diaboli by degrees. There must be places on the earth where such figures congregated, or else escaped to, cringing beneath Civilization's shadow for want of the strength to subvert it. From some extant nook of his heart he would proffer this strength unto them. There was salvation in evil, as in solitude. He would redeem these ultra rejects from the Summum Bonum in the marrow of their marginalization, through the squeezed sac of cankered Catholicism – extracts of Evil, compounded out of existence into enduring essences all their own.

How to move and settle into other spaces beside the one he had now made his own, where he could insinuate his poison currents of influence past inimical detection, was the most delicate conundrum facing him after he had abducted and engorged a titanic tally of dog-walkers, strollers and nature-lovers, causing a national panic in the process. The Police-hunt was now focused on him rather than the Water-Witch, it now being supposed that she had vanished along with the others anywhere between Hackney and Chingford. But still there was no reported sighting of him, for he so contrived to merge wizard-like with his stolen surroundings as to render himself truly invisible to any search-party. The Police were exhausted, perplexed, petrified even. Rumours of a Quatermass-like quarry were beginning to abound in some quarters, eclipsing long-entertained fears about the Beast of Bodmin, etc.. Though the absence of ectoplasm, smoke, flashing lights and visible devastation clearly divided the sceptics from the believers! Some hideous, vampiric serial killer was a marginally more probable scenario. No Name Now's preternatural cunning had acquainted him with the semiology of urban geography, the locus of a language. He configured signposts and noticeboards, maps and designs. He visually and mentally devoured scrapbooks and papers found on his victims, before bodily ingesting them or discarding them with a kind of impulsive ennui. He also took some of their clothing, intimating the uses of disguise. He saw his face in water many times – clawing its reflection till the mirror of Identity finally dawned in his consciousness. And then he rose up to the full stature of his potentialities.

FIVE

With his pursuers scattered and stuck in their narrowing circular tracks, No Name Now – as he may as well be called in advance of self-nomination, if only to suspend the tedious polarity of He/It – stalked a nocturnal passage deep into the tender, unsuspecting Heart of England, where he lay low awhile, feeding solely on the rotten fruits of the earth and the odd bird or animal. In the heated vegetable-swamp of his brain he was seeking an Alter – a rustic outcast, instinctually closer to the beasts of the field and birds of the air than an urban counterpart, wild yet helplessly weak in comparison to himself, with some arterial vein of erudition still pumping beneath the emaciated husk of humanity. Terror being the threshold of initiation, the ensuing pact could help foster his literacy and the other's metamorphosis. The Anti-Christ could then double as a Scholar-Gypsy, and the grimy Gentleman of the Road could become an agile Avenger. But ragged reincarnations of George Borrow with copies of Rousseau's Confessions in their pockets were rather thin on the ground in late Twentieth Century Britain. The ruminant Romany had died with W.H. Davies et al. What ragged trousered misanthropists would yield up their minds as meat to his all-consuming curiosity? He would have to wait and see.

He didn't wait long in fact. He didn't of course know it, but he was settling near the centre of rural Oxfordshire in Larks to Candleford country en route to a radar-glimpse of the proverbial dreaming spires of an Alma Mater he could never have called his own. The odd derelict dreamer wandered the pretty, picturesque landscape, either mourning their remoteness from the Citadel of higher learning Jude fashion, or else cursing its Orthodoxy in the creative bowels of a Blakean Heresy. One such appeared one morning, his dusty greatcoat spotted with dew, hobnail boots peeled grey, hair-shirt tied with string, an abstracted air transcending facial dirt. An opened beer-bottle protruded from a large pocket – the other pocket being apparently empty of Great Literature – its spillages colouring a waterfall of beard, creosoting a tinder-dry mane. The freedom of the land was his – as was the freedom of the City for antler-wearing Aldermen – patrolling his Patria without drill or uniform, in steps that never completed their circles. A penniless, prospectless Pariah, no-one could touch his freedom to be mad and survive. The sun streamed through trees of liqueur onto his dripping face, a gift of gold to dry his alcoholic sweat. He was past account, counting only himself. When No Name Now stepped out swiftly from behind a hedge to stand in his path – a staring Titan, entreating awe – he stopped only as he would before an apparition like any other in his repertoire for a moment. Then he rubbed his eyes, a puzzled seriousness clouding his face with the sobering realization of an apparent impossibility. This was no phantom or hallucination. A truly terrible entity had just manifested before him, as palpably real as Matter itself – and yet the breathing evidence of the Supernatural on Earth. The demon-drink had not this time delivered a demon. A demon had delivered him from drink. Fear gripped and shook him like an enwrapping, suffocating sheet.

He collapsed slowly to the ground, cowering and writhing in paroxysms of mortal terror, exhaling muffled shrieks of mercy. No Name Now found in that moment the means of suppressing Instinct with Intelligence, stepping with gentle power and an alien curiosity toward the gibbering body. Towering directly above it, peering through the coals of his eyes at a victim he would collect and not consume, he then lowered himself until his face was only inches away from the living object that would connect him with the ways of a doomed species. Breathing a film of filth over the man, he struck him into unconsciousness with a stilled stare. Then he picked him up off the ground like some light piece of baggage and strode off deep into the surrounding woodland. When he came to a clearing near the ridge of a slope, he placed him with a curious ceremony in the long grass as if laying him to rest in a coffin. The soft shock brought the man vaguely to his senses, swooning in brilliant light – configuring the real dream of the dream reality/the dream reality of the real dream/in the perpetual waking sleep haze of hung over recollections and imaginings. He started, only to realize the futility of escape. He had not died – he had been strangely taken care of, it seemed. Perhaps he would survive this hideous encounter after all. What to do? What to say? He shifted himself quietly as the monster now in charge gazed out over a sea of flower-crested fields with the magnificent air of a minotaur in repose.

Who are you? What do you want with me? The man managed to stutter, posing the obvious, yet mesmerizingly significant queries to his cosmic kidnapper. When the latter, alerted to the sounds alone, turned its head to affront their source, the tramp shivered in the apprehension that no meaning was registered – no language did they share! And yet through the terrible, non-human countenance, a distinct yearning shone strangely out toward its captor – the urge to become human perhaps? The drunken misanthrope felt his mind clearing, his battered, sunken, rare intelligence surfacing through the falling mist of tremendous delirium. An extraordinary experiment would have to happen if he was ever to recover his freedom from this fiend. He would have to communicate with the incommunicable, educate the ineducable, and receive what in return? Mephistophelian powers? The Faustian pact had long obsessed him, God's having abandoned the world – if he ever existed – to human tyrants demanding sacrifices none of his ilk would ever make, and so the wilderness had claimed him like one of its own in prophetic antiquity, beckoning him to its farthest boundaries. In his sodden desolation the friendship of the Devil seemed attractive, his only hope of dignity – not salvation, not redemption – and the restitution of his intransigent Self. Evil was at least real – here and now before his very eyes – whereas Good was a thankless chimaera. Why squander benevolence on an ungrateful Race? Better to despise it instead, it would never be worthy of its higher pretensions. Only cowardice had prevented him from embracing Satan. Now he felt eerily compelled to contend with the latter's Apostate on Earth, to guide him and be spared in turn – for daring ends?

He raised himself up onto his elbow and gradually steadied his own reciprocating gaze into the face of his silent and temporarily motionless abductor. He saw in the next few moments that the monster before him possessed enough human characteristics to have once been born of Woman – and was not Christ himself born of Woman? So why not the Anti-Christ too as an epiphanous opposite? And his feral grotesqueness may have been bred as much from privation as from the Mark of the Beast. Blake's Nebuchadnezzar came to his mind, and the Ghost of a Flea. The Biblical myths were twisted into another time and place through the physiognomy of the creature, and yet with no obvious parallels in source and manifestation. The stigmata were lacking, and the other symbolic deformities. No Name Now was symbolic of precisely nothing, a great quirk of Evolution. If he could find his voice, he could spread a Gospel truer than Christ's. He could subvert the Species infinitely more than any mere Church. The Dark of the World would come into its own true element at last, its power unstoppable in the momentum gathering to propel it beyond all millennia. He, Syfert, would serve as the weak Virgilian guide through the Underworld of human life, preparing the ground for his suprahuman protegee to take the whole world in his taloned hands and then crush it into extinction. But before any of this would be possible, they had to carry further the beginnings of their trust by finding a means of communicating. Mere ostension seemed grossly insulting to the native intelligence of such a grand and magnanimous-looking creature. Imitating animal sounds seemed even less appropriate – resulting in his swift extermination possibly. Silence seemed closer to the mark, a kind of wordless communion passing from eye to eye in an extended space of mutually magisterial thoughts. A certain world-weariness might be shared in one look, or a rare anger in another, a singular determination in yet another or a lofty resolve – and so forth. The Language of the Look was the key to their tryst.

In developing and sustaining this mode of communication over time, they discerned all manner of subtle gradation of meaning in particular inflexions and gestures of the eye in its facial surroundings. Sound had seemingly become redundant, till one day while venturing across a field in pursuit of a wild meal, they were stunned by the sound of gun-fire. "Down!" Syfert cried, forgetting for a moment his new-found friend's unusual capacities. No Name Now shook his head slowly, then opening his encrusted mouth suddenly uttered the distinct word 'No!' It sounded like a mythical injunction emanating from the belly of the great Pagan Earth. For one instant seeming like an eternity, Syfert was struck more by this monstrous miracle of speech than by any impending danger. But then a man came into his line of sight, a farmer probably, holding a shotgun in a cocked, horizontal pose. Some Oxfordshire farmers still possessed the mindset of their eighteenth century tenant-forebears – spot a poacher, and bag him! As for two poachers – one for the gibbet, the other for the pot! But this farmer was in for a supernatural shock of sorts – short-lived as his remaining breath. For No Name Now then broke into a run, gaining uncanny pace as he closed the gap upon his human food. The farmer attempted briefly to aim his gun and fire again, but found his body swiftly jellifying with terror and his mind hallucinating with derangement. As he finally met his chaser's gaze, realizing in that last moment his grotesquely unnatural provenance, he dropped the gun and tried to run away, but found his feet stuck to the ground like lava. With a greater than Herculean strength No Name Now took him in his grip and pulverized his bones, then carried his lifeless body back with him to the spot where Syfert cringed and stared with horrified amazement.

"You spoke!" The latter spluttered, still more preoccupied with this shattering fact than with the spectacle of the mangled corpse tucked beneath No Name Now's arm like some quotidian piece of luggage. "Were you deceiving me all along, or have you just discovered your tongue like a gift of Babel? Enlighten me, Man! Unburden your mind of its secrets!" The silent stare returned to him of such quizzical hardness, vitiated his leap from elementarity to eloquence. "Eat!" came the voice again, as the farmer's body dropped from No Name Now's hand onto the ground and rolled toward Syfert. "What?! You can't be serious, Man! I may have fallen to the bottom of the pit – but – but I'm not a cannibal!" Syfert remonstrated, addressing No Name Now as if he were unambiguously human for the moment – an old drinking-mate, perhaps. With an imperceptibly swift movement No Name Now was down and at the corpse, tearing off huge swathes of flesh then cramming it all down his grotto-like gorge of a mouth. "See?!" he exclaimed, turning his eyes yet again upon the poor Syfert, as if it were the latter who required elementary instruction in the arts of adaptation to the prevailing conditions of existence. "Oh, no – surely it may not come to this!" he cried out, knowing full well the urge to consume the half-eaten contents of take-aways thrown in waste-bins, having not eaten a solitary scrap for days. In extremis, he would eat human flesh – as no doubt would anyone else, in so far as their very survival depended on it. But he wasn't so far gone – yet – in his own process of dehumanization as to be capable of contemplating such an act without still experiencing a certain visceral shudder of disgust. He couldn't reckon with the compulsive need to partake of his own species – and moreover, to relish it as he did so. He may have grown to hate much of Humanity, but so far his avenging tastes didn't extend beyond a stealthy hyena-hunt for discarded fag-ends or fish and chips.

No Name Now's sudden imploring of him to break one of the ultimate taboos of the moral membership of the human family was so hypnotically repugnant as to threaten to wrench him out of the very casing of his central nervous system. It was true that he was very hungry – he hadn't eaten a half-way decent meal in years, and had just recently survived on odd bits of farm-refuse. The stigma of consuming the flesh of a fellow human held less horrors for him than the sure prospect of death at the hands of his chameleon-tempered kidnapper. So with great unease, he reached a decision to cross over the threshold of a new and terrible territory. In a sense, his prolonged dereliction had always been preparing him for this or for some such extreme barbarity. His moral fetters could hold him no longer though, as he lowered himself down toward the cooling feast of flesh below. Blood oozed through gaping tears in the clothes, caking the furrowed flesh. What if the dead man had had some lethal illness communicable by blood? Syfert finally pondered. Oxfordshire farmers must be the least likely risk-group for HIV infection, he reckoned – though they could easily have been infected by the B.S.E. agent. A mad cow could hardly be worse than a mad man, he concluded – or a quasi-supernatural monster.

Finding a comparatively intact and unstained piece of flesh in the lumber region, he fumbled in his copious pockets for a knife he had carried for longer than he could remember. It was pretty rusty now, but what was a bit of rust compared with what he was about to consume? He had originally kept it for his own protection. Some use it was to him now in that capacity. Opening out the blade with difficulty, he breathed in and closed his eyes momentarily before cutting into the corpse with a gingerly disgust. His hand trembled violently as he raised the first fatty slither of epidermis towards his quivering lips. Then it was inside his mouth, his teeth closing on it like a cyanide capsule. His almost hallucinogenic anticipation of the taste – along with the tobacco and ale-saturated patina of grime encrusting his teeth and gums – precipitated something of an anti-climax, a surprisingly bland flavour creeping through onto the residue of his palate, only vaguely suggestive of a sickly fattiness. He swallowed as quickly as he dared, fearing a fit of choking, but even more the toxic release from protracted chewing. He would entrust the burden to his stomach, his hitherto failsafe repository of the assorted filth from polite and wealthy human animals' waste-products. Bracing himself for an irruption, he caught No Name Now's glancing eye to the accompaniment of a further utterance: "All!" The irruption never came, but his whole body deadened at the injunction. "No,

Man! You cannot demand this of me! What Satanic impositions are you capable of?!" No Name Now shot out a claw, vicing his neck to propel him up like a rabbit, suspending his gibbering mass in mid-air. Syfert knew his helplessness in those few eternal moments as never before, resigning himself with the virtual satisfaction of an ultimate perversity to the inevitability of his fate. He must eat to live was a precept given the sickest twist of all. In the grip of this foul demon's magic, he would survive.

Lowered to the ground, he felt suddenly gifted with blank mind as he tore himself through a surgically tasteless meal of larded gibbets. When he had finished, his beard was stained a bullish crimson and he felt the legacy of blood would remain on his lips forever. An uncanny, savage calm spread through him, and he felt taller – more possessed of powers. An insinuation of strength had passed between them, through some imperceptibly subtle conduit of initiation. He could have sworn something like a smile formed on the face of his invigilating captor – a smile of estimation – that had nothing whatever of sentiment in it, only an empathy of Evil. No ordeal in his life had been as self-transforming as this, with the promise of great freedom after the torment, not the abandonment of his history or the suffering since. His star had shattered and fallen to earth when the Scholar descended into Society – fuelled with transcendent zeal, only to recoil from the rocks of Reality. His failure of courage in the face of rejection had been the source of guilt withdrawing him further than ordained, beyond the pale of his banishment. His ideals became poisonous curses racking the daydreamer or life's virgin. No recovery was possible, familiars retreating in shame and impotence. The prophylaxis of the bottle was all that was promised to him, after taking to the Road that led nowhere in ever-widening/narrowing circles of social and self-estrangement.

But now the Saviour of the Damned had crossed his path and delivered him into the innermost Circle of Hell, safe beyond the reach of punitive Mankind's clutching hands. No taboo remained to be broken, the way ahead was smoothed for fallen angels to be avenged on their banishers and so to reclaim the glory of a pride that knows not the judgement of peers. For this he would do anything. He would eat his way through the whole bloody carcass of the collective species he had been condemned to live among and suffer at the hands of, in return for the taste of an emancipation sampled only by the Olympians among men. For this he would prostrate himself before No Name Now to worship him without irony as the Great Guru of unspeakable license. The Beast had charmed the wasp.

SIX

Syfert had passed his first major test of initiation into the Colony of Cannibals that was soon to proliferate across the length and breadth of England – or to begin with at any rate, Oxfordshire. A more trusting, confiding relationship developed between them – No Name Now revealing a surprising vocabulary culled from sundry sources to feed a self-evolving mind, while Syfert took him to a remote part of the surrounding countryside where he had burrowed underground to create a shelter safe from prying eyes. He described it as a pauper's version of Prospero's Cell and clearly regarded it as a secret wonder of the world. He did not know that No Name Now had spent most of his existence on Earth inhabiting just such a space, albeit above ground rather than below it. Apart from the barest modicum of implements, it contained only books. Not one of these books had been bequeathed or bought. They had all been found or stolen instead, over more years than he could exactly recall – twenty five at least. His aim had been to so encompass himself within a library, as to inhabit it like a stretched skin – an involucrum of perpetual hibernation. This aim had of course proved marginally impractical, as books could never nourish his body in lieu of food. And there was only so much space available for rations, so he would have to venture out into the no longer so green and pleasant land beloved of Blake to build up his stocks – a process which took two to three months each year. And it was during this period that he had encountered No Name Now, while drunk on a Publican's charity in a spring-water desert. He was known to some in the County, but no-one knew exactly where he laid his head to rest under the stars – presuming that like any other gentleman of the road, he slept wherever he happened to find himself after his legs grew heavy with weariness from each day's haphazard pounding of the bye-ways in unbounded rural pastures. The Constabulary knew him as a harmless eccentric – always dirty and smelly and frequently drunk, but never posing any serious threat to anybody or anything. He was so outlandish though, that they didn't wish to approach him too closely to find out any more about him than they knew already, which was practically nothing in fact. They satisfied themselves that he lived like any other rural tramp – and barring the occasional nod, wave and word of cheer, did not seek to extend their acquaintance with this strange, doomed figure any further. Rumours abounded in some quarters about his distinguished background, but nothing could be substantiated by anybody. As for his routine thefts, either he was too practised to be seen or else a blind eye was turned to the necessary antics of a starving man. He never begged or accepted charity, preferring the hardship of his own procurement to the subsistence of a society he despised. As officially he lived nowhere, Welfare was out of the question – even if he had wanted it. Hemlock was preferable to Dole-Geld.

His voice was even more distinctive than his person, a quintessentially august sound that rose from classical depths to strike dead the common chatter of the Age – perfectly articulating the speech-forms of the by-gone Baroque. The words of forgotten authors were his friends and companions as surely as significant others were for the gilded insiders of conventional society. He knew no significant others – save No Name Now. The latter settled in the space like a feral cat curling up in its rediscovered womb/tomb. Syfert covered the entrance with a huge, customized wooden screen, that had ferns and other weeds stuck to it, giving it the appearance of undergrowth. No-one had ever disturbed him in this space that served as Home – not even another wandering outcast.

He was beginning to feel strangely protective towards No

Name Now. For though the latter could kill him stone dead with a single flash of his Evil Eye, the fact remained that there would soon be a widely orchestrated hunt for this Frankenstein Monster *de nos jours*; and only he, Syfert, was sufficiently ignored in this part of the world at least to give his Angel of Deliverance the protection he needed from his pursuing army; and so the scope to fulfil his destiny, whatever that was exactly. And he aimed to find out, to give to No Name Now the words that could articulate what his deeds would later accomplish. He would introduce him to the world of books, which he felt certain he had never once set eyes upon in his life – let alone been taught to read. His guest started to conduct his own investigation, fingering the worn spines of Syfert's tomes as though they were suddenly encountered sheer surfaces to be tested for their solidity. The notion that they contained anything to be absorbed by quite another mode of attention had not yet struck him, even though he had already engaged in a sort of primitive registering of configurations of squiggles contained in other found objects besides books as such. He turned to Syfert for guidance. The latter acknowledged his appeal, and removing a book from one of his makeshift shelves, opened it up slowly and revealingly in front of his eyes. A strong glint of recognition of printed words – and their power to excite – flickered across No Name Now's face. As he peered closely though, he was struck by differences between the language he saw displayed before him and the language he had struggled with on discarded slips of paper he had picked up in the Lea Valley. That was because the language was not English, but Enochian – or a script allegedly transcribed in the terms and symbols of a supra-terrestrial/astral language/tongue, by obscure scholar-priests at the Court of King Solomon in Ancient Egypt. Syfert had obtained, in his characteristic, light-fingered manner, from a dusty barrow outside a forgotten bookshop near Oxford some years previously, an ostensibly early edition of the notorious Necronomicon – the text that had supposedly driven Lovecraft insane.

He had studied it assiduously ever since, and had reached the conclusion that Enochian was a genuine language not of human origin, rather than just a portentous piece of mumbo-jumbo concocted by a bunch of conspiratorial illiterates. If the Book of Revelations had been a gift of prophesy granted to St. John the Divine – and for that matter, the Koran a dictation of the Word of God through the medium of the Angel Gabriel to Mohammed's scribe – then by the same token, Enochian had been a gift of tongues to those either ready or chosen for it by the Old Ones, Guardians of the Unnameable lying beyond Good and Evil. Syfert had perhaps selected this text from a vast range only half at random, being half-convinced that he had encountered a Being – however illiterate – for whom Enochian had been intended, and who maybe knew the language already in some imponderable region of his Intelligence. The ideogrammatic character of Enochian symbols would besides prove an excellent starting-point for Syfert's trepid Education of No Name Now's bleak Genius. He could communicate with him far more surely in this language than he could in English, which he felt was as alien to his new-found friend and companion as is the language of birds to the average human. And yet No Name Now was as much of a free-born Englishman as he, Syfert, always proclaimed himself to be. England was the land – the Patria – where he found himself, whatever his antecedents and nurturing. And if he had never had the slightest notion of the State that prevailed in his Land, he must have identified with the still-enduring wilds of England as surely as any wolf-man with a forest. The State was an abstraction, an abortifacient, that had no place in the natural order of things and the simple scheme of human existence. No Name Now was the instinctual instrument of the Anarchy which Syfert had always espoused, without being able to carry it forward into the sunlight of triumphal autonomy.

It suddenly struck him that he had no name for his friend. The idea that such a monstrous quirk of evolution – or transcendance – had ever been named by anyone, or anything, seemed utterly ridiculous somehow. The need for a name was the felt prerequisite of human dignity, over and above the mere act of identification. Men went to the dogs without names, and where the hell did the dogs go to? But this Being settling into his hide-out was so magnificently OTHER to the Human Race, so rawly self-sufficing, as to render any familiarizing appellation wholly redundant. It then occurred to him to give him a name in any case, a name that would paradoxically contradict itself and the whole business of naming – a name that his friend might have chosen for himself if he could have articulated it, and which he could refuse at his whim in preference for another name or silence in the matter of names. No Name Now. The bearer of this non-name of a name would be a nameless Being in a continuous Present, forever beyond human definition. Syfert had cherished this supremely outlandish condition for himself, but wished to bequeath it to One worthier of its mantle and more capable of enacting the Essence of which it partook.

When he summoned the Other for his Initiation into an Identity above all Identity, he was met with an uncannily knowing look of speechless comprehension – as if the Unnameable One were responding to a call from within its own Universal Nature. NO – NAME – NOW! came the Catechistic answer, with a Mephistophelian smile that subtly and sinisterly undermined the question itself. Approval was not forthcoming, nor disapproval – merely a pre-emptive enunciation of an antecedent truth. Syfert had a way of addressing his friend without encapsulating him, and the latter had another way of communing with himself at the heart of Heresy. The ritual that was not a ritual ended as it began – Syfert having communicated his name likewise, a Satanic title he had made his own in the mists of receding Incarnations – and they regarded one other with a fresh understanding, as if only just introduced by a third party symbolizing the Invisible Host in an Unholy Trinity. Food and drink did not need to be offered as a facilitator of friendship in the circumstances. They had fed to satiety already on the flesh and blood of a human serving as wafer and wine in the Unholy Communion, inaugurating the Colony of Cannibals that would soon over-run Humanity like an insuperable Vampiric plague. No Name Now had a sense of space denied him in the besieged fortress of his Hackney-Home, and lay back on a copious ground-rug like Sardanapalus presiding over a harem of drooling female slaves. Had there been baskets of fruit nearby, he would assuredly have eaten them DOWNWARDS. But the atmosphere secreting in the draped and book-lined chamber would provide him with enough aetherial food to gorge on for many aeons to come. The aroma was heavy with the hung years of sweat and vegetation, lamp-oil and alcohol. Infused into this blend were faint, stale traces of shed skin and burnt incense. The lay-out itself was largely free of clutter and junk however, indicating a curious, cultivated disinterest in THINGS – the ruling obsession of the Water-Witch. It resembled an autodidactic pauper's imitation – or emulation, rather – of an austere aesthete's ivory-tower. The scholar-monk in Syfert had concentrated the essence of the art of abstraction/the abstraction of art, into this realm of his own privacy.

Now that he had acquired a taste for human flesh and blood, Syfert would require no more to trudge across the Oxfordshire landscape in the hunt for diminishing rations. No Name Now would bring home the bacon whenever the need arose. A tremendous feeling of relief swept over him, as if a death-sentence had just been lifted. Even his addiction to alcohol could be overcome – the dilution of despair its sole function. The vigour of the bestial would rid him of despair, perfecting the means to self-sufficiency beyond the reach of the Dispossessed. From his Home/ Headquarters a world-plan would emerge, conceived in alien secrecy and executed with mercurial insinuation. He was off the spectrum of surveillance, a forgotten mole burrowing in from the outside having long ago burrowed out from the inside. His information and facilities were obsolete, but his method and resolve struck at a source of untapped power. The War being prosecuted in his Den – or his head – was already much larger than he was, gathering a sweeping Subterranean movement of its own, that at a critical moment would trigger and precipitate a Cataclysm, belying in its devastation the subtle, invisible force orchestrating the process in the background. Ancient Power never lost its import and purport, however apparently outstripped by the innovations of Techne. The least probable focus of circulation could prove to be the most potent mainspring of unrest. Syfert's mind was the exact counterpart to No Name Now's physiognomy. If both co-existed in the same Being, that Being would be far more terrible even than Moloch the Devourer.

Scientists could follow their paths ad infinitum – building the perfect machine, the perfect robot, the perfect computer, the perfect weapon, the perfect poison, etc.... But Syfert, originally a Classicist by training, clung to the conviction that nothing could ever truly outstrip the power of the human mind itself to influence – potentially at least – everything that happens. The human brain – the principle, though not necessarily the sole seat of the mind – was without question the most complex organism in the Universe, any Universe. And it would always remain so, Syfert thought, as revealed by its obscure Algorithm defining the limits of the Possible. His ESP alone could stop Science in its tracks, if only he could unleash its hidden charge from inside the vast unused capacity of his own brain. No pioneer-Panjandrum of Artificial Intelligence could ever reach into those recesses of his innermost sanctum known only to himself, and then mimic or reproduce them ad nauseam within the wired entrails of some wretched MECHANISM! The mythical Gods of Antiquity were more real to him than any piece of Cybernetic junk manufactured by some degraded specimen of Humanity. The Gods were the actual, projected forms of the Protean stirrings in the Hemispherical Underworld enjoining Man and Cosmos. Their symbolic significance may have altered through Time, yet something of their essential grandeur arising from the elemental endured in all the turmoil of thought that threatened to topple them from their Olympian pedestals founded on shadows.

The Dark Gods were the ultimate rulers over all, the promises of Light unfulfilled in the finality of extinction. A measure of eternity may well be vouchsafed to those organs of corrupted life able to thrive on the black wings of astral intelligences, fanning the Infinite Void/Abyss with the energy and breath of slime and ash. Through his studies and travails in the Lore of the Necronomicon he had wedded himself by slow degrees of initiation to those mighty, beating wings, which at the lowest and highest frequencies of their all-destroying potencies resonated through the entire fabric of Creation itself. On many an occasion had he voyaged out beyond the earthen confines of his hovel-citadel into the unending velvetine stretches of the Astral Void's nocturnal cloak. Only hunger, thirst and cold brought him back to his planetary lair, his physical body still tied down by Gravity and Evolutionary decree to a dried up fount of sustenance.

No Name Now, by a wicked marvel, was as fleet-footed as Hermes and as serpentine as Satan. He contradicted the Laws of Physics, a phantom in fleshly guise. How could he be armed with knowledge he already in a sense possessed? Knowledge is Recollection, Plato held – presupposing the truth of Re-incarnation. How could the slate of Consciousness be wiped clean and a new form of Being emerge, as if from nothingness? If God – that bastard-phantom! – could have kick-started Creation from within his own self-sufficient Being, then so also could Satan spin the reverse of Creation, which could be infinite, from the coils of his own Ontology. No Name Now was, by extrapolation, *sui generis* – the *fons et origo* of Evil, confounding in his antecedence the infinite regress of the Natural Cycle. Knowledge therefore – likewise wisdom or understanding – was transcendental, going further than Plato, deriving from the First Cause/Foundation of the Manichean Multiverse in which the possibilities of Good triumphing over Evil and vice-versa are cancelled out, yielding an amoral hierarchy of parallel universes without end. Only this was a Hierarchy of Self-Rule.

SEVEN

The following weeks and months were spent in the superfluous 'Education' of No Name Now, punctuated by occasional forays into the countryside to feed off human victims, in which no trace or speck was left of them. They had simply gone out walking – and disappeared off the face of the Earth! The pattern of course fitted that of the disappearances in the Lea Valley – a fact that didn't escape the attention of the ailing police-teams assigned the task of tracking down the monster(s) responsible for this virtually unprecedented spate of serial killings, both in terms of scale and savagery. Their searches had therefore extended into Oxfordshire. But No Name Now had in the meantime refashioned Syfert's hide-out into a Hermetically sealed quasi-Pharaonic mausoleum, and the Police had detected no sign of its existence from above the ground, even though they had passed very close to the site. They were more baffled and bewildered, exhausted and demoralized than before. And yet with a National Alert long since orchestrated, the pressure on them to redouble their efforts in preventing the carnage from achieving epidemic proportions was intolerably great. Some of them were now privately of the view that they were dealing with something truly non-human, while continuing publicly to defer to common-sense and rationality, if only to try to stem the mounting wave of panic and alarm.

Syfert's accumulation of powers had proceeded apace with No Name Now's mastery of both English and Enochian, each language seeming equally strange to him, like any other language –

and yet as innately familiar as the lost tongues of Babel's fallen Tower. Syfert had impishly remarked at one point that Enochian should fare rather better than Esperanto had as an International Dialect! Though from the frown of incomprehension on No Name Now's face, he reckoned he'd over-stepped the esoteric mark. The Enochian Tablets after all, had been the preserve of a priestly caste – a rarefied elite – and No Name Now seemed to have an awareness of this. But he would learn from Syfert that the circle of Elitism and Democracy could be squared – indeed he knew this already in the deeper regions of his cast out nature. Much of Humanity may have to be consumed in the fiery breath of Pagan purification. Nothing could alter this course, if the Damned were ever to be freed. The Blessed were already too corrupted, in the crassest sense of the word, even remotely to deserve being spared this inexorable fate. But the remaining survivors – the Race of old, risen anew – would elevate True Democracy far beyond the most-trumpeted achievements of the Ancient Greeks, like Aristocrats of Gargantuan liberties striding across the smouldering Earth in tune with their songs of Singularity. And Syfert would strive to belong to their number, clinging at first to the serpent coat-tails of his prodigious protegee – then standing erect, like a mountain in his wake. No Name Now, having had his fill of human flesh and blood, would grow above Prometheus to consume the nectar of liquid sunlight.

When his education was completed – or so stimulated as to enable him to steer it whither he would – Syfert wanted No Name Now to go out into the world like Zarathustra stepping from his cave, and initiate those other Syferts of the world into his secrets and his powers while destroying their enemies or the rest of Mankind. On a smaller scale, Syfert would be charged to do likewise. If this process could be timed to coincide with the end of the Millennium some years ahead, then the Apocalyptic potential of this nihilistic explosion all over the Planet would in his estimation be vastly increased. The Second Coming of Christ would be simultaneously subverted and upstaged. Millenarianism was of course a nonsensical creed, but the power of superstition could be turned to the advantage of an infinitely more revolutionary, Antinomian movement. Chesterton had been right to say that when people stop believing in God, they don't believe in nothing, they believe in anything. However, God was still very much a part of the equation in the phoney Decade of Evangelism. God had become the imbecile's best friend, the fanatic's global persecutor, the lunatic's inner voice. To paraphrase Chesterton, people now believed in any brand of God like soap – or a good many did. If anything fundamental was going to emerge from the religious, moral and cultural decay of Post-Modern Civilization, then it had to engage the ruling passions of the vast majority of Mankind – however phoney they may be. Evangelical superstitions were deeply superficial, yet they drove much of Humanity like a herd of Gadarene swine over the cliffs of common-sense. But what if this mass-hysteria could be re-directed away from Religion, towards a kind of Politics – a monster-Politics, as Syfert called it? This was a sort of Direct Action taken by some new breed of Grotesques, coming into their element and challenging ordinary, decent Humanity with its presumption of the rectitude of nice virtue.

Such an outcome to the accursed Twentieth Century would be almost worth dying for, but for the fact that the metamorphosis it entailed might promise immortal life. The countervailing faith in Reason and Science would furthermore be supplanted by the faith in phantasy growing out of existential faithlessness. Phantasy had to be tested to destruction, to squeeze out of it the bilious juice of Truth. To Hell – or Heaven rather – with the unattainable realm of Objectivity! Make manifest the ultimate realization of Subjective Phantasy! This was Syfert's creed. And nothing – but nothing – would deflect him from his bent. What the world had appeared to resemble when filtered through the alcoholic haze of his downcast vision, it deserved truly to become when he finally rose above it into the hallucinated Space of astral flight. He had at long last done with deranged escapism and was prepared for a concentrated, penetrative assault against the raised Fortress of excluding Society. His stepping stones on the flooded Causeway to Self-Possession and Self-Efficacy, had been the Names of Power contained in the Profane Book – Cthulhu, Hastur, Nug-Soth, Yog-Sothoth, Nyarlathotep, Barzai, Ibn Ghazi, Dho-Nar, Shub-Niggarath – which he had never made the error of supposing to be anything other than mere symbolic invocations of something essentially nameless that lay behind them. This nameless source was what mattered above all else, and ultimately he could only merge into it by means of the abandonment of ALL language – even Enochian, the symbols of which had been translated first into Arabic and then other languages, which enabled odd copies to fly the nest of secret Archives by virtue of a calculated stealth to end up serendipitously in the hands of persons such as himself, or so he had affected to believe.

The book could have been an invention of Lovecraft's, of course – spawning an industry of rogue-copies of an 'invisible' original. Or if it had been a genuine vision of the mad Arab Abdul Alhazred, as his studies had rationally persuaded him, it still remained in the final analysis one among many cipher-tools for the use of dislocated avengers. But it had seemed to him far superior to most others of his acquaintance, including the notorious Grimoires banned by the Medieval Catholic Church. The Ancient Damascan Outcast had been diabolically inspired, the dried canals of his desert-soul opening up to receive black streams of unearthly wisdom, the original cryptic keys to the Enochian Tablets. He, Syfert, could make what prophetic use he would of the ritual injunctions and ceremonial incantations, having added his own poetic refinements to the text in translation. The mysterious rubric 'That which is not dead which can eternal lie, and with strange aeons even death may die', which heads the text, haunted him on account of its incompleteness. He had sought to render it grammatically as 'That which is not dead can eternal lie, and with strange aeons even death may die.' But the removal of the second 'which' subtly, and disturbingly, altered its sense. So he had changed it to 'That which is not dead which can eternal lie, (spells/enters/inhabits/moves in) strange aeons when even death may die.' But the removal of the word 'and' again failed to do justice to the original, or what he could only take as the original. So he had waited for his supernatural muse to come to his aid. It did not disappoint. He had ended up expanding the two lines to four. 'That which is not dead which can eternal lie, and with strange aeons even death may die as when breathing creatures thrive upon the night, resurrects in the shadows cast by the light.' Not perfect, but the sense was more roundedly revealed.

Fearing at first the descent of a curse for daring to add – however slightly – to the wording of such a potent script, he had soon realized that all texts without exception are in some measure palimpsests and tissues of corruption. Every man is at liberty to amend any text that is handed down to him. Indeed he must do so – if only by virtue of the necessity of exercising his own faculty of understanding and bringing his talent to bear on the creative furtherance of texts. So Syfert's very personal reading of the Necronomicon was tantamount to a new version therefore, his secret simulacrum of an unfinished Chronicle. He reckoned himself to be a greater poet than Alhazred and all the Translators put together. He could 'key' into the essence of what had become his own evolving text as well as any Ancient or Modern, by-passing whole reams of mumbo-jumbo to alight upon its elliptical elements. The two meanings of 'spell' thereby became one. His conceit was cosmic.

Invoking the Gods – the Old Ones – was supposed to be done under very specific astrological and seasonal conditions, but Syfert thought this an arbitrary and artificial constraint imposed by self-regarding ritualists blinded by the mystique of yore. It ought to be possible to invoke all the Gods in a single, concentrated form, under absolutely any conditions whatsoever, by practically any means and for any purpose. His purpose was purely evil, or even beyond evil altogether – the ultimate negation of all. He had been, in a sense, engineering No Name Now in slow stages – based on his own deviant interpretations of the Necronomicon rituals – long before he encountered him, as if he had appeared before him by means of his own conjury or as a sudden, final manifestation resulting from a protracted period of incubation.

His 'black beast' was before him, yet come from another source and sufficing. Cthulhu had coalesced spontaneously into No Name Now, through randomly read runes. As a supreme instrument of the vengeance of the Damned, No Name Now need never preside over his 'Race' like a High Priest of the Profane Path held above the ordered echelons of an hierarchical caste. He would stand alone and apart, along with Syfert and all his Acolytes – Anarchs of the Astral. Enochian was a preferred Code for the assembling of Powers to be distributed among the discarded atoms of abandoned life-forms in an irredeemable Universe. Syfert had never belonged to any sect/cult/order/church/brotherhood/movement of any kind – not even before his self-banishment into the wooded wildernesses of Old England. He had always walked alone, nurturing his night-creeds within his own solipsistic sensorium. The greatest Beings never joined anything. The Church of Satan was a contradiction-in-terms, if ever there was one! No true Satanists would ever allow their powers to be checked by membership of any forum of alterity. Satan himself was only a facilitator of his own superfluity to supremely strange Beings such as Syfert. Evil was always diluted when it became established – respectable!

Aleister Crowley had been little more than a posturing clown in his time, frittering his few talents away in the hunt for notoriety – the tat-queen of Occult finery, finally dying perplexed as a tweedy provincial. The 'wickedest man in the world' was a joke on a back page, a mere sop to risible vanity. He couldn't have harmed one of Dennis Wheatley's rabbits. Yet of all so-called Twentieth Century Maguses, he was the one who had supposedly called the solemn Satan's bluff and wittily spun his own heresies. Syfert had never been impressed by either his example or his following. The most potent Magus of the Twentieth Century was completely unknown, yet pre-empted scepticism. He had unnamed him.

The Risen One was now more or less fluent in speech, devouring – mentally – as many of Syfert's texts as he could fill into the time of day and night. There were of course numerous

Latin and Greek Classics, Hebrew and Arabic scriptures and Oriental tomes, in addition to the aforesaid Enochian and English. Also there were secret histories, works of occult philosophy and 'Higher Science', as Syfert described them – though few orthodox writings on Theology or mainstream volumes of History, Science, Philosophy, etc., as he had never rated these very highly. The applications of Pythagorean Mathematics to Neo-Platonist Mysticism and Metaphysics were of great interest to him however, as were Alchemical journals or work-manuals drawn from the Corpus Hermeticum. His contempt for Exoteric Science had so prejudiced him against almost anything written since the beginning of the so-called 'Rationalist Enlightenment' from the late Seventeenth Century onwards, that his shelves were all but bare of any such texts. Syfert was happier living in the Age of Merlin than in any later one. And as even Science had chased its own theoretical tail through Time, maybe long past ages would soon revisit the Earth and no longer need to be revisited themselves. He was certain that Time could be split open and salvaged, just like Space.

One aspect of No Name Now's intelligence struck Syfert with clairvoyant force. He did not appear to need to be taught by rote. Indeed, what may have appeared to be a characteristic handicap encumbering hypothetical wolf-men – namely his unsocialized, not to mention unhumanized, unspeciated alienness – precipitated the most remarkable leaps of comprehension in him, from complete ignorance to instant absorption. And his sense of what mattered to him and what didn't, appeared to dictate *a priori* what he learnt and what he ignored – nothing else mattered. The knowledge he thus acquired would not only power his Project in the World, but also camouflage his savagery in a period of preparation. The ability to move through Space without causing alarm or even being noticed – hovering at the boundaries of human traffic, oscillating between concealment and revelation – was a necessary concomitant not only of his survival, but also of his penetration through the heart of Civilization. After a year of monastic devotion to his Education, punctuated by odd outings to ensure his provision, No Name Now was as ready as he would ever be to go forth and prosecute his Curse. Syfert likewise had developed the strength of a hundred men and the swiftness of a supernal beast. They were lost to the Powers-that-be, demoralized in disarray, and found to a calling as imminent as it was ancient.

EIGHT

In addition to the spread of a semi-invisible breed of metamorphs, a colony of Headquarters sprang up in places underground or in remote dwellings where whole families and communes were annihilated or else mutated into hospitable hosts. The most furtive and feral threat to Society was extending its feelers forward from the hinterland toward the arenas of open thoroughfares and the citadels of surreptitious control. Syfert introduced No Name Now to his Society of Fellow-Outcasts – old Avatars re-united or new ones *deja vu*. Their burdens were well and truly weakened in being shared. Syfert, with No Name Now's assistance, sealed up his infernal Base as a time-capsule – to be returned to occasionally, but otherwise left in the hunt for captive terrains. He changed his appearance, abandoning his aged clothing for a surreal suit of grey while trimming his tundra-beard to a goatee V and shaping his hair into a tarantula-thatch. The purple decay of his facial skin faded slowly as the mad lustre of his eyes sharpened with Mephistophelian clarity. No Name Now donned the dignified courtesy of a restrained beast, replacing his slime-logged patchwork quilt of corporeal cladding with a clean swathe of cloak and shawl. His unchanging satyr-features were cunningly obscured by a hood and scarf, enabling him to spirit himself down any busy city-street without drawing a policeman's eye. He was now a magical infiltrator at large, an ubiquitous *agent provocateur*, a star-fiend shooting through Society's sky to raze its members in a blinding eclipse. For the next few years, He and Syfert trod their own leys in a Pilgrimage of Disgrace.

Their method of secreting themselves into the walled confines of their enemies' strongholds was to steal into homes in the early hours of mornings, exterminate and consume the inhabitants, settle at their leisure and move on. Sometimes they would spare their victims, bestializing them at a stroke before releasing them like armies of deserter-ants to follow their urges as they wished. Countless homes were left empty and silent, no visible or audible clues arousing suspicion regarding anything out of the ordinary that may have happened. Ghost-villages in remote rural regions appeared without attracting outside notice. The emptied spaces slowly filled up with the progeny of a nameless Race, quietly plotting the Destiny of Nations. Soylent Green and the Invasion of the body-snatchers had nothing on this! These Stepford Wives had rather more on their Agenda than looking cosmetically demure and docile whilst wheeling shopping-trolleys around provincial Supermarkets! Their burgeoning Community of Interest was underscored by Anarchic flood-paths of Individuation. Little outbreaks of Vampirism were occurring in the most unlikely places – even Tonbridge Wells! Sub-Cultural ferment was blamed as usual, and for once it was true – albeit with a difference. The American Gothic and Voodoo cults were spreading to Britain and other parts of the world, like some snake-virus feasting off the surviving filth of the *Fin-de-Siecle*. But until they encountered No Name Now, none of these amateur Satanists would know what Omen had passed in answer to their inverted prayers – or not, as the case may be. The most depraved abomination emerging from the swamps of the southern States would not possess an iota of the potency gifted to the mysterious protegee of the departed Water-Witch.

No Name Now was so seemingly ubiquitous, his shadow remained in places that he had long left behind – and his presence in any one place and time embodied the Epiphany of Evil. While knowing nothing of the latest Science of Surveillance, he was effortlessly capable of evading the most advanced sensor-devices available to the Police and Security. There had been a little-reported case of this happening some years before in Highgate Cemetery, when the Police had set up a net of vigilance that was supposed to be inescapable, to identify and trap some reported 'entity' they presumed must be human or animal, but which led them to consider other possibilities when it continued to evade them. They were convinced of its existence, but concluded it must be something unearthly – not a ghost exactly, but more akin to a Golem. This was in the wake of the publication of 'The Highgate Vampire', in which it was claimed that a hideous, black creature with red eyes had been magically created or invoked during some ritual in the Cemetery, which had terrified the seasoned Satanists present right out of their tiny, credulous minds. Whatever credence or otherwise may be attached to this claim, enough people took it sufficiently seriously to involve the Law, which also had to concede that something inexplicably murky had been happening. The Roman Catholic Church still maintains that the Devil is a kind of animal, and not just a Supernatural Angel existing in spirit- and image-form alone. Not that one should necessarily attach too much credence to the claims of this great Tyranny perpetuating the Roman Empire by other means. But the Sophistical subtleties of Catholic mystics still hold fractionally more appeal to this author than do the dogmatic certainties of secular Materialists. Such beliefs can also perhaps be squared with Evolutionary possibilities arising out of unexplained gaps in the Fossil Record and the failure of Scientists to lay the Lamarckian spectre finally to rest.

Be this as it may, the fish caught by Syfert was bigger by far than all those paraded by the self-appointed, 'highest' Occult organizations on the Planet – from the Maitreya and the Emin to the Coven of Anton Sandor La Vey. All these pre-millennial tunnellers in the pyramids of their puerile phantasies plumbed the shallows of the Psyche, oblivious of the vast Bomb assembling in the depths beneath them. At the arbitrary, but appropriate moment at the end of the Millennium, the long-stored and withheld charge would finally be released and would blow all these jewel-thieves right out of the water – along with everybody else. It was so long now since Syfert had been inside houses – or buildings of any description – that such an experience seemed to belong to some very remote incarnation in an endless chain of repeated lives. In the language of the new Power in the Land – of which Syfert and his conspiring fellows remained aloofly ignorant – he had not felt that he may have some potential STAKE in Society since abandoning his formerly promising heritage. Although the stake he felt he now possessed was more of the kind employed by vampire-hunters, except that HE was the vampire waking to disarm his enemies at sunset and turning the sharp-pointed instrument around to aim it directly at the heart of Society. If No Name Now was the stake, he was the driver.

No Name Now may have other ideas of course, like Frankenstein's monster, except that he had no human creator to blame for his burden of exile. Moreover, Syfert had encouraged his facility of speech instead of damaging it to the point of virtual destruction in a deadly game with transplantation and electricity. He would be all alone at the critical moment, yet not by virtue of betraying his new-found friends. One of these friends inhabited a huge, Jacobean pile inherited from his family along with a financial legacy substantial enough to subsidize a life of leisure. He had then vowed never to do a day's work in his life – nor to obey a single order – but to cocoon himself away from the world in a state of Hermetic luxury denied to poor Syfert. He had then collected not books so much as animals and people principally, along with all the aesthetic adornments of his home appropriate for the cultivation and constant stimulation of an amorally refined sensibility. The animals roamed freely in acres of wild and overgrown land, including exotic peacocks and feral cats, while the people lived as they pleased in the eerie spaces of the mansion, a mobile menagerie of human freaks of no account whatsoever in the outside world. The occasion of this man's first encounter with No Name Now and Syfert was predictably dramatic, with horrifying screams of imported and home-bred sables and cervals being torn apart and their blood guzzled before being eaten whole reaching the ears of the inhabitants late one night as the march of the Anti-Christs stole across their Estate, precipitating a panic-rush out into the gardens as suddenly repulsed by the presented spectacle. The sheer remarkableness of the man's aspect however – and that of the members of his coterie – ensured their survival and subsequent conversion to the paths of ultimate, efficacious powers. The cannibal-poachers quickly assumed pride of place at the heart of a Grand Guignol house-hold, lost and forgotten in the haunted Arcadia of Dorsetshire. Their host's name was Edwin Clore, a Scion of the Sinister.

He wore his black, grey-streaked hair long – reaching more than half way down his back – his face being beardless and pale, marked by an aquiline hauteur as befitted his demeanour. A severe Dandy, he dressed only in dark-coloured, late Victorian, velvet, silk and satin costumes. He spoke with a dry gravity, as if his mouth were continually filling with ash that soaked up his saliva. Althou- gh over six feet tall and still only in early middle age, the skeletal fragility of his anatomy suggested a body being claimed already by its corpse from a future time. An almost visible, tangible aura of Pagan antiquity and Seigneurial perversity hung about him as he sat in a plush, ornate, high-backed chair in one corner of his dowdily decadent, sprawling space of a drawing-room, surrounded by his company. Syfert instantly recognized in him an equal and a virtual spirit-double. The only real difference between them was that of wealth. Their life-long delvings and visions had been pitched on the same elevated plateau of rarefaction like twin-tracks converging on Infinity. Even No Name Now was impressed, picturing before him a Being he would once have devoured with a casual ferocity assuming the grandeur of Zeus in treading underfoot the mediocre mass of a Species that had spurned him in its mindless indifference. There was clearly much to converse about and deliberate upon with this Epicure. Syfert resolved to treat this palace dedicated to the nefarious as the Grand Central Headquarters of the assault on Modern Civilization, from which all the lesser outposts already established could be secretly co-ordinated in their collective offensive. But he had no wish to offend his new-found friend and confidant, whose delicate dignity struck such a wounded chord in him.

He was certain he could involve Edwin at the very core of the Project, after revealing to him the extraordinary significance of the disguised monster he had arrived with, or rather so cavalierly invaded his kingdom with. Their pursuers would never trace them here in this green outback of sleeping nostalgia. Meanwhile, their numberless cohort-cells scattered throughout the Land would continue their advance upon the Body-Politic like a plague of Necrosing Fascitis, mentally self-programming in the physical absence of their original inspirers.

Edwin graciously passed over the business of his guests' unconventional mode of access to his Estate and the manner in which they had disposed of some of his animals. Though being fascinated by the nature and aesthetics of cruelty, he was deeply curious as to how such savage creatures could have been killed with such consummate ease by what appeared to be a couple of humans – albeit humans of a remarkably singular sort. He himself was too physically frail and neurasthenically afflicted even to raise a hand to the more mischievous imps in his midst. Yet mentally, he was consumed to the point of intoxication with the imagery and atmosphere of the most extreme varieties of violence. If only his wretched body were healthier and fitter and stronger, it could then respond to the frantic, frenzied, fantastical messages from his brain. No Censor existed in his cerebrum, nor cerebellum. No moral code applied within the boundaries of his kingdom. He was a commanding spectator of wild perversity at its least restrained. Like Syfert, he had sought throughout his life for the instrument of his Evil Incarnate in the Other.

The possibilities of the Supernatural absorbed most of his inner energies, leaving him depleted after prolonged flights of phantasy in which he strove to connect his body with his mental object. It appeared as if his blood were slowly draining out of him with each effort at transmigration that he made – into what? A void of evaporation? A vessel of astral intelligence? An Olympian Ubermensch? Perhaps even without his new friends' special assistance, he could have achieved his goals. Yet with their assistance, he felt he could achieve truly awesome miracles. He introduced his guests to his coterie, each of whom bore some radical peculiarity of a physical, mental or spiritual kind. Some of them he had gone well out of his way to discover, cultivate and accommodate. Others he had encountered by chance and had established an instant and lasting rapport with. Yet others had come across his kingdom on their searching travels and had been drawn ineluctably by its rapacious magic. All of them in their different ways had been seeking the artificial paradise suggested in Baudelaire's line, 'Anywhere, anywhere out of this world.' The physiognomy of Edwin Clore's Estate resembled that of an old Anglo-Saxon Region — a little Wessex or Mercia preserved against Progress, ruled quietly by the mysterious Pendragon-figure at its centre. Rumours abounded about him on the lingering Hardyesque Grapevine of the most conservative County of all. Yet few people dared venture anywhere near his privileged patch of Earth, preferring to leave him be in his lawless realm.

The gardens were splendiferously littered with titanic hybrids of weeds and plants, impenetrable undergrowth and scrub, swallowing woods, hedge-mazes, wild grassy stretches, untended ceremonial lawns, eroded grottoes and statues, entangled arboreta, wild-perfumed pergolas, stranded gazebos, petering paths in Gothic labyrinths, etc. Once entered, this sprawling wilderness of broken grandeur had entrapped Edwin's neophytes — as he curiously called them at first — sucking them into his hospitality as a refuge from the hostile fauna lurking chameleon-like in the hypnotic flora. He had groomed each one of them in turn for a specific role in his grey enterprise, otherwise permitting them as much liberty as he did his animals. They were happy to take up their dark-anointed positions in his household, believing themselves to have found not so much a Guru or a Master to follow and obey as a Great Emancipator of their hidden dreams and innermost desires. He imposed no ritual or ceremony upon them, expected no deference to his authority, and indeed positively encouraged their strongest anarchic impulses to grow stronger still. In these respects, he magnetized them by the grim exuberance of his Soul rather than by any Patriarchal rigidity of Example. Mystery, not Dogma, was the binding force between them. Not that there was in any sense an 'open door policy' operating in Edwin's Grand

Free Hostel for the ill-assorted Outcasts of England. Only La Creme de La Creme drawn from among this lot would ever survive the perilous trek from the Boundary-Gate to the Mansion-Door, to be received with an aetherial grace into the heart of the Kingdom. The animals saw to the rest.

There were at present around twenty of these Elitists of Esoterica 'squatting' in the Mansion, each occupying a separate chamber of his or her own in the vast sleeping quarters on the upper floors. As there were only very rarely deliveries of food and drink – the Squire having alienated all but two of his Family's traditional suppliers – they had had to assist Edwin in cultivating organic produce in his gardens, weed-soup being a speciality of their home-cuisine! Edwin never ventured beyond his Estate, physically. All his wealth was contained inside his house, and he owed nobody anything. All the maintainance was self-supplied – candles and oil-lamps sufficing for light and fire-heated kettles for boiling water. The *sine qua non* of Antinomian autonomy was always of course Economic self-sufficiency. And as Syfert and No Name Now could tell them, it helped if you could eat anything! Not that Edwin and his people lagged far behind their guests in this matter. Although they had a cultivated horror of consuming animal flesh – inspired by Edwin's reverence for the savage grandeur of the Bestial Kingdom – and hadn't seriously contemplated human cannibalism, their vegetarian predilections were so bizarre they would have converted even the strictest Vegan to the delights of animal fats. And just how bizarre their tastes were their guests would soon discover, for Edwin summoned them all to the Dining Room, where a typical household meal had been prepared and laid out for them by some willing members of the assembled company. The long oak table could readily accommodate fifty people, so more than half of it was unoccupied when everybody took their seat. Edwin sat at the top of the table, more out of hospitable courtesy than through any insinuation of rank. No Name Now and Syfert were invited to sit on either side of him, like guests of honour at a formal banquet, while the others observed no particular order in claiming their own places.

The table was covered in a profusion of foods, resembling the mushy contents of Monet's murals. Each dish was a pot-pourri of different flowers, weeds, plants, fruits and vegetables mixed according to the secretly improvised recipes of the household. In one vast earthenware pot fox-gloves, cowslips and ragwort had all been crushed into a paste liberally decorated with fungi and elderberries. In a tall jug the extracted juice of dockleaves had been poured, as if to provide a soothing counterpoint to the heated raw nettle broth. Fresh stripling juice was on offer to wash down plates of soil-cake and wild nuts. This was a new departure for Syfert – and even for No Name Now, whose repertoire of natural feasting had been confined to the cruder embarrassment of riches afforded by the Hackney marshes, the Lea Valley and the wilds of the English Counties. He hadn't ever enjoyed the cornucopia of rot flowering in the Rococo thickets of a Landed Estate. Still – if Rasputin could stomach arsenic, then stripling juice should offer an easy test of resilience for any cannibal worth his salt.

NINE

Among Edwin's company were a mystic lost to his own Laws called Solarius, a ranting firebrand witch called Elethea, a deranged logic-chopper/number-cruncher called Aleph, a diabolically extreme writer called Obscurius and a silent Sylph called Antarctica. There was also a blacklisted scientist called Dr. Plague and a murderous conspirator called the Annihilator. All their names were self-concocted and nobody cared or even knew what their or the others' names had been originally. They had systematically forgotten their pasts, if they had ever had pasts as such. Each inhabited his or her own separate sphere like a primed force-field, ready to explode into neighbouring spaces. Only Edwin's majestic magnetism held the harmony of opposites intact. As everyone fed and drank themselves to satiety on the organic meal with a difference, Edwin pontificated with a far from Papal piety for the benefit of his guests on the character of the gathering and its proceedings under the roof of his household. "Of course," he intoned with a macabre dryness and thin loftiness, turning to face No Name Now then Syfert, "You must not imagine that what I'm presiding over here – if I can be said to be presiding over anything – is in any sense a cult or a sect, or indeed a group of any kind. So individual are we all it is as if each of us inhabits a mansion of his or her own, for this house is well and truly a Palace of many mansions – if you'll pardon the paraphrastic Biblical allusion. Such is my contempt for communes of every description, that if I could be said to have a single house-rule for the people assembled here, it is that they must at all times rigorously eschew communal life. But then such is the calibre of each of them, I scarcely need even to insinuate leave alone emphasize this condition of my hospitality–." The august irony of his voice trailed off in clouds of rhetoric, conveying to Syfert the visionary impression of a dark prophet speaking from the Ancient of Days. He smiled knowingly and took up Edwin's dangling thread, as if he were continuing a conversation of his own.

"You can safely assume that my companion and I share your prejudice in this matter, and no more seek membership of a commune in your house than inclusion in the Orwellian Hierarchy of the Modern British State. We – like yourselves – are Outcasts, and unashamedly proud of our partly or wholly self-chosen predicament. Moreover we are Outcasts with a vengeance, waging war on everything and everybody standing not only in our path as such but also in the path of a crushed multitude craving the absolution of licentious selfhood. Though if you'll pardon my jesting paradox, this exquisite feast of filth laid out on your Table could only have been prepared by virtue of a pre-established harmony among the members of your household." Edwin caught Syfert's puckered smile on the uprise/uptake, interjecting swiftly with a further tangential spin.

"There I must take issue with you, friend. Your paradox is a nice one, though not difficult to resolve – or dissolve, as the case may be. The apparent orderliness prevailing all around you is an elaborate charade, staged not for your benefit as guests but for our benefit as resident-voyagers into spheres of influence disconnected from the physical arrangements of this household. With the merest rudiments of order in place, the refinements of chaos may be enjoined without interference from outside. This is an elementary practicality only, requiring no artificial or arbitrary Division of Labour. The co-operative instincts of the Human Species are precisely what drives its individual members apart. So with a minimum of distraction from the barest necessities of Life or Nature afforded by the improvised economy of elements displayed on this Table or throughout the Household, the freedom of each

Individual here to fly away into the rich vastnesses of inner and outer space is thereby facilitated to the maximum degree. Indeed, the inversion and subversion of supposedly normal eating customs provides an exact refutation of the Law of pre-established Harmony, proving that any shared or common instinct can be reversed and undermined with sufficient ingenuity and application. This is one part of the whole business of being an Outcast." He gazed at Syfert with an unearthly gentility, that matched the primeval ferocity of No Name Now in its (im)pure unfathomableness. The look reminded Syfert of Odilon Redon's remarkable painting of Mephistopheles, which he had seen once in another rarely recalled incarnation. The Evil emanating from the face pervaded the viewer with an infinite, half-smiling subtlety, from no one specific point or source but in an irresistibly soft, all-encompassing manner – a cursing charm. Edwin possessed an elective affinity with that expression – if not the appearance of the face itself – Syfert noted, taking up his cue again in their spiralling Satanic discourse.

"But the reversal of a principle simply invokes another principle and so on *ad nauseam*. If the aim of each one of us – and my companion and I are not your mere guests – is to push the tendency of the Individual utterly beyond the Fabric and recuperative power of Society or any Collective Order, then the fact of our being together in a shared space is bound to counteract that tendency at a microcosmic as well as a macrocosmic level. And what better analogy is there for a Society in miniature than a gathered assembly of persons at a Dinner-Table? The difficulty of the Atomistic Project as I call it, is brought most clearly into focus in such a setting. For each individual present is not only pre-defined as a social member in the widest sense, but is also governed by the implicit or explicit rules for the preparation and use of a Dinner-Table. The food may be inherently disgusting and unpalatable to any normal members of Conventional Society. But we too are conforming here to an inverted mode of consumption by participating in a meal which has been prepared by some of us in a shared effort for all of us to eat in a mannered parody of a civilized party for the moneyed elite." This measured diatribe drew a soft ire from Edwin, who expostulated very slightly. "But the meal has only just commenced – and the others present have yet to announce themselves. You could scarcely imagine the subversive twists and turns that forever transform a mere meal in this household into something undreamt of in Plato's Symposium. We could of course sit alone in corners with food on our laps, or separately raid the gardens at random intervals. But that would be both obvious and tedious. And the fact of our all sitting together at this table to indulge a natural appetite we share, in no measure limits the possibilities of any one of us turning the presumed ritual completely on its head – not physically necessarily, but verbally or intellectually. I would be as happy inhabiting this inherited pile all alone as I am to share it with these kindred-spirits, but each of them would assure you that the mansion is no more than the parts of its sum, to juxtapose an epithet. Is it not so, Aleph?" The one addressed looked up from his mess of leafy potage, a soil-stained red beard rising up after the face to triangulate its black eyes focusing like star-light just reaching earth. "Define part and sum, then I shall extrapolate for you," he said suddenly and simply.

"Very well," Edwin demured with a weary grace. "A part in MY sense is an atom escaped from a whole and abandoned to itself, while a sum is a mere conjunction of parts never amounting to a compounded whole. Extrapolate from that if you will–." "You deviate delinquently, yet boldly from standard definitions logical, mathematical, statistical," came the icily restrained response, followed by an abrupt departure, "and so I will concede to you a th- eorem requiring no proof, that the mansion does not exist when I alone exist as a subset of the transfinite set of my selves." His eyes appreared to withdraw the light from Earth back into a void behind all stars. "And why does the theorem require no proof?" Edwin gently inquired. "Because when written out to Infinity, it is complete. To the objection that I cannot have enough time – or paper – to write it out, I really don't need to reply. In the Transfinite Calculus, it can simply be ASSUMED that the time is available. But unlike Gregor, I have found a short-cut enabling me to justify my definition of 1 as 1, and 2 as 2 and not 1&1. And as I am also 1, and Solipsism is true in all possible worlds, then 2,3,4,5....n are therefore redundant and so you and all notional others do not exist." His eyes narrowed as if shrinking to a point of zero mass-density. "Ha! But WHO is the ultimate Solipsist?!" interjected a third party – a murkily epicene figure like a cross between Strindberg and Struwelpeter, with a squawking, shrill voice, no other than Obscurius – "You can play your endless games of tiddly-winks with Number-Theory, but ultimately numbers are just illusory abstractions, meaningless squiggles! Truth is Metaphysical, not Mathematical! And only I can falsify it with my OWN Truth, which is far too obscure ever to write down. My Book of Books is composed entirely of aetherial mould, the configurations of which would blow Jackson Pollock's mind from here to Infinity and back! It's an invisible spread-sheet of my neural fungus!"

"NUMBER is ALL! You mirage-freak!" Aleph thundered at him, as if only the optical illusion of his antagonist needed dispelling. "NO – NIHIL is ALL!" Obscurius shrieked back at him, re-conjuring the illusion of his existence from the malignant springs of his adamant opacity." "Now you're trespassing on MY terrain!" another voice pitched into the exploding fray – that of the Annihilator, clad in black from head to toe, his face a cubist prism of shadows and scars. "Nothingness must be created as though it had been all along, the perfect non-state that only an Anti-Being such as myself can restore to itself for Eternity! Just imagine that – the nullification of all that is, or appears to be, in the ultimate STRIPPING away of everything not absolutely fundamental, the SUMMARY EXECUTION of the Puppet-Gods gyrating on their pedestals above our little existential side-show in a cosmic cess-pool! What could be purer and more beautifully logical than that – the final vindication of Physics, Poetry and Philosophy?!" His voice rose to a terrifying crescendo of Damoclean defiance, the Russian spirit wedded to the Olympian. A frozen silence ensued for an indeterminate period, interrupted quietly by a voice of such silken serenity it threatened to immerse the assembly in Elysian sleep. It was now Solarius's turn to speak. Dressed in a long, soft white robe, his hair and beard seemed to merge indistinguishably with its coloured texture, a waterfall of the Spirit flowing stilled from the whites of his eyes.

"There is nothing to destroy in what has never been created. The Sword of Vengeance forever glances off the blade of grass – and then, its edges blunted by the energy of its own wind, it becomes as one with the blade of grass and vibrates with the rest of creation in a symphony of echoes and a dance of light. There is no God – nor Devil neither – but an infinity of suns flaming the darkness and burning without extinction. We need not worship them, but partake of their rays and float in the silver spectra of transfigured worlds." Hardly had his honeyed tones evaporated on the air, when Elethea burst forth from her coiled cocoon of impatience to strike another discordant note in the progressively deranging Dialectic. Resembling Rochester's wife freed from the attic, her hair and nails destined to survive the longest reincarnation-cycles, she spat and hissed her animated venom at the World represented around the Table in the huge old mahogany-panelled Hall bedecked with fading portraits and decaying trophies – the unchanged legacy of Edwin's titled forebears, scions of the House of Usher that would never burn down, its ghosts perishing in the flames, lasting as the perpetual monument to the concentrated, yet spreading aethos of the Eighteenth Century Hell-Fire Club patronized by Count Dashwood.

"I have heard nothing except the repeated chords of miserable men's cries resounding through the ages – the failed, frustrated whines and groans of inferior specimens of a superfluous sex! When will you all realize that everything men complain of stems from your failure to control the power and mystery of Women? We are the source and object of all your quests, aspirations, goals, fantasies and hostilities! We guide and govern you like magnets of devouring seduction! Nothing you feel, think, say and do occurs without hidden promptings from US, the Occult rulers of the planets and the stars, the singular Sex ordained by the secret Scribes of the Ancient Blueprint dictating all things! You men are an Evolutionary afterthought, developed for our amusement as an alternative to lesbian loneliness – an irrelevance we don't otherwise need! We will never labour in Lethe! The Underworld is our playground and you our victims!" She cackled with fierce abandon, her eyes glinting with an unearthly light all their own. The other women present glowed and pulsated with an animal affinity for this untameable scorpion of sensuality. One appeared unaffected however, her bloodless face an ice-cap sealing her mouth stiff. The surface-frost cracked as in a sudden thaw and speech escaped from her lips like a trail of ammonium breath. Antarctica provided a cold counterpoint to Elethea's feline fire. "Woman is extinct – like Man. I embody the new Species, with the metabolism of the Immortals. I am passionless, as I am deathless. There is no future for the sexes, only the metamorphosis of cold Logic. When you inhabit the poles of Existence, you become like me – a warrior of the wastes, an ice-dagger stuck fast in the heart of Humanity. Vampirize your blood and become STRONG – survive the death of the Sun and outlive Time itself. Follow my example or die with those who feed on feeling. Only stone-cold flesh can endure in worlds where hope is forever abandoned. The best revenge is perpetuity." The assembly were again silenced by this curse leaking through a raised tomb-lid, a sepulchre of white death. But one other Being present broke the silence – as before.

This was the man known as Dr. Plague. No secret research-establishment on Earth wanted this man within a million miles of its doors. The most abominable covens of biochemical warfare would hold up crosses at his approach. Once a brilliant Scientist, his obsessive interest in poisons disturbed the Authorities to the point where they thought it necessary to refuse him any post or advancement. Malthus and Mengele were his heroes. He then combined his interest in poisons with Black Magic and began work on his own trying to develop a 'psychic toxin' deadlier by far than Anthrax or Ebola. And in the process he made himself by slow degrees immune to one substance after another, starting with Cyanide. He was by now a Plutonium addict, having crossed the threshold that ensured he lived on as something other than a mere human or animal, his skin shining with a dusky phosphoresence, his hair sticking like tinder to his gross, cortisone face. He felt surer than anyone else – with the exception of No Name Now, still unannounced – gathered in Edwin's infernal eyrie of outlasting Mankind, after he had inflicted on it the very worst imaginable atrocities. Satan knew not the depth of past deprivation that had engendered his present depravity, the evil hatred of Humanity providing its own ultimate justification. His voice had a brittle crackle to it, like trapped electricity.

"All your Myths are the stuff of Movies and nothing more. To transform or destroy Reality, you must first of all understand it. Only Science can do justice to the conceits of Magic – the evil soil of Technology, the Garden of Eden corrupted. There is no unknowing of what is now known. And what Science has revealed to ME is that there are no Laws of Nature or the Cosmos that a peerless intelligence cannot re-write and so undermine. If the conditions of Nature can be so altered as to be unrecognizable, then new Laws come into being – or perhaps no Laws whatsoever. If high energy-Physicists can alter prevailing conditions in different space-time regions simply by generating unprecedented temperature increases in those regions, then just try to imagine all of you what I as a pioneering Toxicologist could do with a substance that could not only irradiate every life-form on this planet but mutate and plasticize them into wholly new Identities! I have the means to do this already assembled in my micro-kingdom upstairs, while my macro-kingdom awaits me all around in the great fulfilment of my work!" He gazed about him with a malignant intensity few of the others could match, savouring each word of his prophesy before continuing in his characteristic, drier-than-death vein. "If it is true that all of us here are the maddest free agents in the world today – partly courtesy of Edwin's hospitality – then it is also true that some of us have survived and thrived by virtue of our sheer self-conviction and methodical perseverance, I more than anybody else! For I alone among you have perfected the indisputably feasible MEANS of translating my Diabolic intent into tangible fact! The rest of you are to varying degrees dreamers and fantasists, however dedicated and dangerous in THEORY! But in the final analysis – when the crunch comes – your animus against the World will only achieve its aims by means of the ordinary sort, crude weapons and poisons, etc.. or else words, words, words, the curse of Hamlets down the Ages! The imaginary and abstract ether of your personal conspiracies against all that opposes you, however refined and concentrated, will evaporate away into thin air when the Armageddon of MY making occurs! I wonder why I share the same roof with you all sometimes, but I still recognize in each one of you the closest to a kindred-spirit in six billion or so perishable specimens of Humanity I am ever likely to encounter anywhere. So strange as it may seem, I wish none of YOU any harm – and even strive to further your otherwise vain ambitions with the fruitful blessings of my greater curse."

The gathering fell silent for the umpteenth time as Dr. Plague brought his eloquent Manifesto to a temporary conclusion, passing on to Edwin the cue to summarize the proceedings for the benefit of Syfert and No Name Now – who having listened without interruption to the sequence of speeches, were inwardly preparing to put their own syncretistic spins on this Historic Symposium unappropriated by Bedlam. Edwin exuded a silence sublimely strange for an indeterminate interval, then spoke. "My Brethren beyond all Brethren have spoken, each in turn, encapsulating in a few improvised words the very kernel-essence of their life-long pre-occupations here on earth, *sub specie aeternitatis*. They and the others could of course speak at much greater length – and will do so – or else perform their uniquely perverse Philosophies in this unconfinable visionary space of the Imagination that brings all worlds into being. But their precis will for now suffice to give you the exquisite flavours of their animosities. It falls to you then to expostulate your own designs for a parallel-purpose – especially your semi-invisible companion who has yet to utter a single word." He referred of course to No Name Now, by way of an invitation to Syfert.

Syfert was swift to respond in kind, launching into his rehearsed introduction of No Name Now as the towering hero of the present gathering. "My companion is perfectly able to speak, I do assure you, but chooses not to for reasons which only concern him. However, if I give you advance-warning of his tremendous potentialities, you may almost prefer that he remained silent for Eternity. Though he will speak, when he judges that the time is right. Let me say then that He is the Avenging Titan of the Great Oppressed of all Ages – and I am his devoted Emanuensis, shall we say. He is supernaturally endowed and yet sufficiently human in appearance to pass as yet unnoticed as such amongst Mankind. He is not the Anti-Christ – he is greater still than the Anti-Christ, the Anarch unbounded by all such polarities. He is not sent therefore, but is risen among us *sui generis* to eclipse the phenomenal world in its entirety at the moment of the death-dawn/dawn-death of planetary-human civilization: the Millennium itself! I have been striving throughout my self-possessed existence to elevate myself to this plateau, but could never remotely have achieved such a goal without the serendipitous agency of our encounter some time ago. He has since wrenched my spirit out of its sink of Diabolic delvings into the clear night-air of a proud, terminating capacity. He is the embodiment of what I only glimpsed in my occluded visions. He will eclipse and trump every devil-inspired plot and plan adumbrated at this table with an effortless ease defeating our sense of awe. He has certain physiognomic peculiarities, I warn you. Furthermore, he has no name – it being a complete mystery how he was born and nurtured before I met him. So I called him No Name Now, a way of addressing him with which he seems curiously to concur. And I shall now request of him – if he so wishes – to reveal his face fully to you all and to speak his mind."

So saying, Syfert steadied his gaze level with that of No Name Now, and then nodded slowly, motioning him to part slightly with his secret. The latter appeared to grow in stature for a few seconds without moving from his seat, like a homunculus of himself expanding into its giant potential. Then he removed the shawl covering all but his controlled eyes, nose and flat, fleshless lips. He turned his head to confront the assembly, provoking hushed gasps from all of them, even Dr. Plague himself, who had never witnessed such a chimaera in his life. His scientific fascination with the possibilities of Transgenics had not prepared him for such a spectacle. What appeared to be a hybrid of human, animal and monster was clearly also a product of natural evolution rather than artificial breeding, which was counted a strict impossibility by most if not all Scientists. Hideously deformed humans were aborted at birth, and if kept alive could only survive with artificial support. This fully formed Chimaera appeared superhumanly strong and in no way burdened by its Biological defects. What force other than the Satanic – which no respectable Scientists allowed – could have so conjoined with nature to produce such a sublime Grotesque? he wondered to himself. He rubbed his eyes twice to ensure he wasn't hallucinating – scepticism always had to be satisfied first, then serious work could begin. He wasn't hallucinating. He was seeing a monstrosity of dark myth made flesh. Satan DID work his magic in the world and HERE was the proof he had long been seeking! He had gone further than Syfert even in the pursuit of his own metamorphosis, but still acknowledged that toxic mutation was not tantamount to a species-shift. The evidence of THAT was now before him, and not in him.

"How Wonderful!" he exclaimed, not surprisingly the first to find words for such a moment – with the possible exception of the Annihilator, with whom he had always had the most difficult of relations under Edwin's roof. "And to think I only suspected him of being shy!" he added with an exquisitely depraved smirk. "As the only trained Scientist present, I would like very much to examine him. What we have here at first glance appears to be a living refutation of Darwinism – that damnable CHRISTIAN pigeon-fancier's creed glorifying the mere mechanics of monkeys! I have long harboured and nurtured the conviction that Lamarck was right about Evolution and Darwin wrong, but no other Scientist would ever listen to me! I have proved to my own satisfaction that there are sufficient anomalies in nature to override the mechanistic hypothesis and obviate the vitalist hypothesis instead – except that the vital force is inherently contaminated, of course! I know that just as there is far more darkness in the Cosmos than light, so there is more disease in Life than health. The point is not only to recognize this fundamental fact, but to so inure oneself to disease as actually to be STRENGTHENED by it! This I have done, but only by slow degrees with the aid of toxic substances. Our companion here however is a perfectly evolved specimen of imperfect nature – a true marvel of malignity! With this living monument among us, we can crush Civilizations like soft heads beneath our feet!" Syfert gazed intently at Dr. Plague throughout this impassioned paean of morbid praise and then intervened with a singular counter-blast of his own.

"Much as I am struck by your ingenious devotion to a black end, I think I should remind you that No Name Now here is the guinea-pig of no man, beast, devil or God. He is wholly and implicitly his own master, subject to no Law that you or I could even conceive of. Should he serve to spearhead some collective surge of our various individual projects, that will be entirely of his own volition and nobody else's. If however he decides to strike off on his own at some unprecedented tangent to our notional circle, or for that matter to sabotage our stratagems, there is absolutely nothing any of us could do to prevent him. I assure you. I have cultivated his trust over time, but he could snuff me out of existence with the flash of an eye. If you wish to cultivate him yourselves, any of you, you had better prepare yourselves for REVERENCE! And I jest not. I feel I have only survived and been fortified by his alien grace because he had some purpose initially in keeping me alive. And then I was useful to him in facilitating his gift for Language and learning, and in that soil a fragile tryst was cemented. As for myself, I have long despised the reign of Science and Technology and have decidedly turned my back on the Post-Rationalist-Enlightenment World to recover the potency of the Great Curse of Antiquity. If one believes enough in phantasy, then phantasy will become real. The question is, which phantasy should one believe in? MY phantasy is of the oldest spirits, invoked to swallow the world and be fattened on its wastes. No inventions of Man can match the destructive whims of such unimagined, illimitable spectres of the bleakest Essence. I employed the obscurest and the most nefarious rituals I could unearth for this purpose, but have since abandoned them under the magisterial spell of No Name Now."

At this mention of his moniker, the Great Silent One stirred into speech all of a sudden – cutting a trajectory across Syfert's path. The voice resounded deeply like a low, hypnotic bellow. "I am the oldest of the oldest ones of which you speak, emerging on your planet as a beam from the farthest dead star to return you to its source from which all has come. Distance in Time and Space is as nothing to a universal Being at a particular point. I am here without needing to be summoned, manifesting from the necessity that is freely decreed as a self-spun fate in the self-consuming realm of existence entire. I am the Avatar of Destinies, avenging every Outcast against the Alienators in Authority. The condition of Existence is Anarchy and my self-determined Purpose here on Earth is to restore the Planet with its False Order to the True Freedom that prevails elsewhere throughout the boundless terrains of the Cosmos. Having heard the testimony of each of you, I can re-assure you in your ultimate, cast out predicament that the Power is here with you to wreak havoc and mayhem in the bloody wake of a Diabolical Day of Judgement soon approaching. The scales of Justice and Injustice will be tipped into an Abyss of Nothingness, from which all the Outcasts of this World will resurrect gloriously and forever rid of their Historic burdens. For I too am cast out, supremely so, but in the manner of One residing at a privileged point and holding the Fulchrum with which to balance the Cosmos or else catapult it into the utmost oblivion. Thus my most intimate and unbreakable empathies are with those of whom you are the very Exemplars, and my most forceful and efficacious antipathies are against those who have presumed to erect their ESTABLISHMENTS in the name of spurious Legitimacy enshrining rigid hierarchies on every populated planet. You are not alone in the Cosmos. And whether you join with me or not, you will be vindicated. For I am not Christ, but a Being greater than God for which you have no name in any of your tongues."

The Annihilator could no longer contain his explosive energy, eager to combat the settling awe in an effort to prove his own ascendancy. "How do I know you're not some illusory impostor, Man?! Prove your superior powers to my satisfaction and I shall join my project to yours. What is this Day of Judgement of which you speak and the bloody vengeance you promise to exact? For one at pains to deny he is Christ, you employ distinctly Christian Language. Justify yourself to me NOW, Man – here at this table!" No Name Now bristled imperceptibly at this threatening challenge, an imploring look from Syfert and a placating look from Edwin deciding him against rising to the bait. Clearly, a human Antinomian of such terrifying aspect as the Annihilator knew no fear and had no sense either. Otherwise, even he would assuredly have bowed to his limitations. After a further pause in which he composed himself like an honorary human, No Name Now answered his steely inquisitor peaceably and to the point.

"When I speak of a Day of Judgement, I do not mean it in the Christian sense – every day could be a Day of Judgement, in that sense. I am not seeking to call human souls to the Bar of Divinity at an appointed hour, but will rather choose a day of great, albeit meaningless significance to humans, to enact an irreversible decree of my own that will destroy the carapace of so-called civilized life and then regenerate in a new form all that is buried beneath it and of absolutely no account in the annals of your History. As for how I shall achieve this, it shall be done by the most ancient of means – single-handedly of course, with or without your blessing and co-operation or that of anyone else for that matter. Syfert has already referred to the Millennium, and it will be on the final day that I shall act through the gift of the mightiest cataclysms of all. The Power is within and without, but it transcends the sword of Christ as surely as it does his healing hand. My Language, like this Power, articulates origins prior to any Bibles written by Man or God. No Bible could contain me, not even the Book of Enoch." At the mention of this, Obscurius pricked up his flapping ears and intervened. "Eh? Which Book of Enoch are you referring to – the well-known one or the unknown one?" "The Book of Enoch," came the imperturbable reply.

"Either you're being Gnomic or you're being obvious. And only I hold the keys to Gnosis –" "The Book of Enoch." "Saying that three times doesn't make it true, even if you're Gertrude Stein in disguise. And she was a lesbian fraud, in any case–." "He's referring to the Enochian Language, revealed in the Necronomicon – the ultimate, profane book." Syfert chipped in on No Name Now's behalf. "Oh, I see!" Obscurius exclaimed, chuckling throatily to himself. "Well – I wrote my own version of THAT aeons ago and lost it in a public lavatory I seem to recall, though I can't be absolutely certain. Some tramp probably wiped his arse with it and succumbed to a fatal dose of occult poisoning. Thus the residue of my work lives on in some unmarked grave – fittingly OBSCURE, wouldn't you say?"

"I used to think nothing forbade my ridicule, till I encountered that book," Syfert retorted severely. "Oh – so YOU were the tramp then!" Obscurius continued his impish burlesque, regardless. "As a tramp with a marked preference for primary sources, I never once visited a public lavatory – " Syfert drily kept his composure. "You mean a hole in the ground is a hole in the ground, etc. I might follow you there, if I didn't consider the uses of excrement as a substitute for ink in preventing unqualified readers from persevering beyond the first line of my Book of Books, which is of course invisible in essence, though as substantially repellant as I can conceivably contrive to make it." "Shit's only good for one thing – and that's for burying Govn'ts with, you arsehole!" the Annihilator stormed in. "Ah yes, but that's only its first use. Imagine whole Libraries and their contents composed of fine, liquid ordure drying out to various degrees of hardness. What a Universe of cultures that should be!" Obscurius waxed animatedly, his face radiating a murky shine. "We're straying so far from the point, I'm losing track of the intervening points," Syfert resumed. "That is the point of a pointedly pointless diatribe, in the art of which I am unexcelled!" Obscurius flashed back. "In one of my many essays towards a material text, I conceived the idea of writing in such small script that even readers with perfect vision would need powerful microscopes to decipher what I had written. And then they would discover to their amazement or consternation that I had split up each word of more than one letter into part words according to an exhaustive set of permutations and combinations. I would thereby separate the devoted from the dismissive readers by drawing them into the Sisyphean exercise of making the split words whole according to the only one among thousands of detailed formulaic readings of the entire text that actually makes sense – albeit only to me!" He cackled obscenely.

"And what makes you imagine that ANYBODY should want to persevere beyond the first WORD of such a futile exercise in masochistic perversity?" the Annihilator demanded with barely controlled spleen, adding "writing's a dead art, in any case. In the beginning was the Deed, not the Word – and in the end will be the Deed too, MY Deed above all else!" "Nobody unpossessed of my morbidly concentrated attention-span COULD persevere beyond the first LETTER of anything I ever committed to print – and that of course includes the VAST mass of Mankind! But you're right about one thing, as it happens. Ultimately, the best writing negates itself. But there's an infinite diversity of things into which it can dissolve, and I alone am chronicling its multiple fate in every rotting culture I can procure. A BLOOD-BOOK is a fitting tribute to the senile idiotic Death of the Author, written in Denida's blood – Ha, Ha!" "When you go down with your wretched Book, that will be the most fitting tribute to your imaginary readers!" the Annihilator snapped back. "But I shall outlive my own Oeuvre in the mangled souls of all those weak wanderers lost in the labyrinths of my creations. I shall have the last laugh at Humanity's expense. Genius thrives on recognition, however warped in the extreme it may be. It is not adulation that I crave, but the bitter reckoning of a superior vengeance. The wilderness is my domain, and I shall draw Society into its icy embrace, only to crush it into crystal extinction. I am farthest beyond the reach of Culture's co-opting armies and am testing Truth to the greatest destruction it has ever suffered."

"Define Truth!" Aleph's voice suddenly rang out, aroused from an abstruse sleep. "Why should I? Truth to my mind is so inconceivably huge, even I can only scrape off so many layers of false skin from its ever-elusive body. Truth is an error striving in vain to correct itself was one passing definition that occurred to me long ago. If it is no more than some figment of fiction, why bother to try and define it at all? It will always be too multi-faceted to comprehend by any mind that elaborates it in the process. And what else can it be but a noumenal chimaera?" "Your addiction to metaphor and rhetoric has so twisted your imagination, it has muddled your intellect beyond recovery." Aleph laid down his Law with an unswerving stringency, quite unfazed by the suffocating conceits of a Littérateur. "Truth is a function of Logic first and foremost, and secondly a property of Language. It can be defined very precisely as ascribable to those formulae well formulated in accordance with certain fundamental assumptions, which although arbitrary, allow and enable us to derive an entire logical language from them. And then the conventions of natural languages provide us with corresponding criteria. The same considerations apply to Falsehood too. And so an interesting problem arises – how do we account for Indeterminacy, or that to which we cannot ascribe values of Truth and Falsehood? Can we simply eliminate it from our Calculus altogether, on the grounds that given purely formal requirements only determinate formulae can be said to be well-formed? Or do we have to concede that there is Indeterminacy in the very Concept of Logic as there is in Physics? My patient unravelling of the Transfinite Calculus indicates that contrary to what many have thought, the latter is the case."

"If Logic and Mathematics are Languages, then they are presumably subject to the limitations that all Languages possess, by virtue of being essentially Evolutionary by-products or expressions of the abstract operations of the human brain," Edwin serenely intervened. "And so your Calculus must surely demonstrate that there is an Algorithm governing the parameters of the Conceivable and the Possible, and it can even define what the Algorithm states." "Precisely – you have put it nearly as well as I would. And I have this Algorithm, to the highest power. With this Algorithm, one has dominion over EVERY universe of discourse – a measure of control not even imaginable for all the Medievalist Magicians and other assorted cranks who dream of secret powers, symbols and formulae, but lack the ability and dedication to make real advances in any truly sophisticated branch of learning. Away with Mystique – the man who comprehends the Logic of Number controls everything!" "But how does this understanding translate across into a tangible manipulation of the Real World, or what is crudely referred to as such by all those who lack the intellectual imagination to conceive of a world other than that in front of their noses which they cannot countenance as an illusion?" Edwin persisted.

"That is the wrong way to pose the question. To anybody not possessed of such subtle understanding, only the occurrence of a cataclysm in the Real World would persuade them that abstractions actually work. But viewed from my perspective, subtle changes in the Real World indiscernible to unsubtle minds are occurring continually in parallel with subtle understanding. Once this has been recognized, then the way is paved for serious progress. Just as I can SEE the Fibonacci Series being explicated in Nature, so I can DETERMINE how my Algorithm regulates all the functions of the Human Mind. The *Deus ex machina* and the Ghost in the Machine meet in me, at this defining limit. Refute me if you can." "I refute you!" the Annihilator shouted suddenly. "Mathematicians, like Scientists, attempt to blind everybody with their arcane language. But the fact is they cannot prove a single one of the assumptions on which their theorems are based. We're simply supposed to accept them. If nothing makes sense, then numbers don't make sense. They're just an impenetrable series of self-verifying fictions – that's all they are! Nobody ever proved anything interesting or important or useful with numbers. Only ideas and actions enable us to comprehend and change anything. And the ultimate end of Dialectics is precisely NOTHING – the tissue of destruction! I shall translate my Idea into reality through the sheer power of Negation alone. History doesn't demand this – only Individuals, for whom History is a mere infliction, as is Society, Nature and the material universe itself."

"You are on the right intellectual tracks, friend." Syfert

intervened, "but your only weapons are words and deeds of futile violence. If you wrote a book, like Obscurius here, its influence if any, might be posthumous. If you tried to contaminate Mankind, like Dr. Plague here, it might take a lifetime of odious Technological self-sacrifice on your part. Only with a truly Transcendent gift or capacity, such as that possessed by No Name Now here, can you extend your project beyond the immediate sphere of influence to a larger and potentially cosmic sphere. And so I must re-iterate that our only hope as Individuals – every one of us here – is to recognize in No Name Now our Facilitator, and to absorb from him as I have been doing as much power as we possibly can. Then, in the words of Poe, 'we can set the world on fire'. And this need not – indeed shall not – involve any compromise of our autonomy, but rather a creative pooling of our exceptional inner resources in the common interest of furthering the autonomy of each of us. Therefore, I wish to propose a joint project with the aid of No Name Now which I firmly believe will draw active participation from you all. Please bear with me and listen awhile." "You have our ears, if not our hearts, minds and souls," Edwin cautioned. The whole assembly for the first time synchronised a fixed and attentive gaze upon the infiltrating wizard in their midst, daring him to challenge their anarchic separateness for the sake of a momentous cohesion.

Syfert fixed his own eyes on each pair of eyes fixed on him in turn, before resuming his speech. He was astounded by the curious formality of a Symposium that had threatened to exceed in uncontainable craziness absolutely anything that any other gathering of outcasts from Human Civilization could possibly attain. And yet the formality was like a tourniquet on Truth, squeezing out its sternest juices, concentrating its blackest essence in a forum of unearthly power. If the tourniquet were twisted only a little more, the critical fusion that precedes catastrophic fission would inevitably occur. All great movements have originated in secret gatherings such as this, he considered, incubating the germinal ideas that shape Society's Destiny. But the Illuminati of the Past bore weak fruit, lacking as they did the evil genius that could eclipse Establishments everywhere on Earth. They were too idealistic, and above all too enlightened. They did not cultivate the ruthless instinct driving all successful endeavour, whether for good or evil – or for something higher than both. "I think the time has come for me to confide that No Name Now and I have already begun our work. Before stumbling across your remarkable kingdom, we had for some time been scouring the Country for fellow-outcasts to share in the burden that unites us all and in so doing reduce it. In other regions, there are free initiates spreading their influence as we are here. Others however resisted us and had to be disposed of. The Fascistic implications of this should not concern us, when the freedoms of us all have been so strangled at birth as to dwarf in Fascistic design any amount of retaliatory killing we may commit. And a lot more killing will be done before the hour of our greatest freedom arrives. I know that even the most abstracted and aetherial of you recognize this necessity for your own sakes, if no-one else's. And I can tell you when the aforementioned hour will arrive, exactly – at Midnight, December 31st, 1999. Such a time may seem absurdly portentous to some of you, but I can assure you neither No Name Now nor I belong to any Millenarian Cult.

On the contrary, our purpose is entirely subversive – not merely to usher in an Age of the Anti-Christ or whatnot, a negation of the Second Coming, but above all to revolutionize the Life of the Planet, to create a New Species in effect that is wholly in control of its own destiny. This will require an unprecedented phase of nocturnal destruction followed by an eternal Renaissance of Life as we have never known it save in our most outlandish dreams. There is no more significant date in the near future than the end of this wretched Millennium – at least for Christians, Nationalists and others. So although this date holds no intrinsic significance for meta-humans like ourselves, our best opportunity for galvanizing the crushed forces of the World Order must coincide with this date and no other. Let the antithesis of the Christ and the Anti-Christ resolve itself in a higher synthesis of the Unnameable. Then History will never again be divided up into thousand – or hundred – year chunks, for it will need no Chronology whatever in the living experience of each of us. We will have enemies not only in the Global Establishment itself, but in the ranks of all those sects, cults and movements arraigned against this Establishment and united by absurd Ideologies and Faiths. We are alone – the PUREST destroyers and creators on the planet!

And by what means, you will all be wanting to ask, are we to stage a Millennial coup of such magnitude? My answer is that No Name Now is gifted with the power to spirit an annihilating current or charge through the entire fabric and supporting structures of this and other countries. The force is with him, if you'll pardon my descent into Hollywood speak! And we can assist him between now and that crucial date by helping to strengthen his force and prepare the ground – scorch the earth, I should say. The more momentum we build up in the approach to the Millennium, initiating or else exterminating our enemies, the more our Facilitator's powers will grow. Christians exhort us to love our enemies. But I say, what is the point of having enemies if we are merely to love them? Our enemies are not incidental obstacles to virtue, but proud opponents of equal or near equal stature. Otherwise they are not worth cultivating. We waste none of our inner resources on pitiable, pathetic specimens standing in our paths, do we? So these are not our enemies. Only those Beings and Powers that can actually militate against us deserve the title of Enemy. And we thrive on our opposition to them, don't we? They are not to be destroyed by infiltrating or joining them however. That way leads to Trotsky's death! No. We must remain on the outside, slowly moving toward the Centres of Power by secreting the population of one small community after another into our movement – or else oblivion. Already there are Villages sleeping the sleep of England as Orwell would say, only with a difference – they will NEVER awaken! Our Apostates have taken the place of the previous inhabitants, assuming an air of normality attracting no suspicion from Authorities or as yet unconquered neighbouring communities. Our heroic contagion is spreading with systematic cannibal thoroughness, you could say – and what better alibi than a well-digested victim?

Now if only you're prepared to step outside the boundaries of your kingdom and assume an active part in the propagation of a Great Race of Outcasts, then with the calibre of calumny you demonstrate, veritable quantum leaps will occur in the pre-Millennial surge of forces happening all around us. This magnificent Gothic eyrie is the launching-pad of a great Global assault, not some permanent enclave for the triumph of Narcissus. Every one of you can achieve his or her ambition more fully while acting in concert than in isolation, however splendid. But you must venture out of doors and into the fields of rival kingdoms, if your nutshell-nightmares are to manifest through infinite space in any way other than the metaphor of Hamlet. You must acquire a taste for human flesh over and above the offerings of the soil and green nature. You must acquire the strength of many men and the power of will possessed by the most ancient of Magi. You must have the capacity to make yourselves invisible and to steal your passage like the deadliest of viruses into people and buildings and institutions, every small and large obstacle confronting you and repelling your desire and very presence. There is enough animosity in this room alone to shift the planet out of its orbit. But the Archimedean Fulchrum we need must extend from its origin here to a point above the Earth, if it is to gain the leverage needed to topple Civilization into free fall through Outer Space. If it remains confined within the walls and gates of this kingdom, then it will never serve its function and purpose as it MUST! I should know. I had been imprisoned in the same pursuit for countless years, till I encountered No Name Now.

If we are to form a tryst, then that is only because our individual goals are ultimately identical or so similar as to entail no denial of autonomy in their combination. Or the furthest Goal that is perhaps beyond each of us, so transcends our differences as to unite us all the more powerfully in its thereby attainable pursuit. So the radical proposition I am putting to you all is finally this: Join forces with No Name Now and me in destroying much of the rest of Humanity – village by village, town by town, city by city, nation by nation, continent by continent, the Globe itself; and so create for ourselves both individually and collectively, the planetary conditions we seek for the maximization of our potential, the greatest fulfilment of our destinies. And let the hour we celebrate our victory for eternal license be midnight, January 1, 2000! Let us score not just one in the eye, but one in the gut, heart and soul of the Millennium, and do it in a manner and style that eclipses the pseudo wizardry of the Scientific/Technological Age! Let the Age of the Outcast and the mass of downtrodden, yet dark vision-inspired Mankind risen up like Prometheus and Spartacus before them, only with SUCCESS, be ushered in for an Infinity beyond measurable Time! We have no interest in failure. Our enemies have always traded on our weakness and stupidity. Let us show them that we are far stronger and cleverer than they, and that Power and Authority will be renounced forever after we have completely destroyed theirs! So will you persist in bashing your heads against the impervious wall of Tyranny – or grasp this miraculous nettle I offer?"

His Periclean oration at an end, a period of uncanny silence not unsurprisingly descended upon the gathering. And perhaps equally unsurprisingly, it was Edwin who first broke it. "You drive a hard bargain, friend – like chaos and insanity, no less. I, for my part, am inseparable from my kingdom. As long as I can remain a Law unto myself here, which I am, then I am sublimely unconcerned about the fate of the outside world. My sole concern is that it does not impinge on me. If I can create my own Counter-Civilization, which I have been doing here for a long, long time, then I do not need to destroy Civilization itself. Like Marx's 'State', it will simply 'wither away' in due course. So I am inclined not to follow you in your urge to depart my kingdom, taking my Brethren with you to fight foreign wars which should not concern the highest Beings on this planet. I have no more use for religion and morality than you, nor Humanism neither. But I am not capable of the violence that you demand, save perhaps in the realms of the mind and spirit. But this violence spills into visionary worlds ascending to the upper circles of Inner Space and descending into the lowest. Its impact on Outer Space is subtle, Hermetic. Time wears away at the material world and the cycles of Civilization, patiently doing the work of the Astral Intelligences pulling the strings of Fate. I fancy I am the embodiment of the very highest of these Agencies on Earth, though I have no pronouncements to make from on high in the manner of Moses. The only Commandment I offer is to break all Commandments. And therefore I speak only for myself in refusing, albeit in the vein of empathy, your request. But others here may respond differently."

"Indeed I think they will" Syfert retorted. "Dr. Plague and the Annihilator for example, are as consumed with raw world-hate as No Name Now and myself, even if their chosen methods differ from ours. Even the women have the makings of true Wagnerian assassins! Far be it from me to break up your Brethren, Edwin. But you cannot prevent any of them pursuing their ends further afield. Though they may return some day to this Great Headquarters in Hell, if it be the truest spiritual home amongst the many they may stumble across during their travels in the mythical lands of the Giants become real. You will remain here, proud and inviolate – a remote beacon shining forth darkness from an impregnable source, while your rogue-satellites trace the orbits of their own obliterating stars. It is a logical extension of what you have been incubating and procuring in this household since its legacy fell into your hands." He turned away from the self-effacing Lord to face the Brethren. "So then, who among you will join us and leave this cosmic spider's nest you have made your home and conspiratorial base? You must make your decisions soon, as neither I nor No Name Now wish to outstay our welcome here. We shall leave tomorrow morning before first light, crossing country at enormous speed en route to our next territorial conquest. Some of you may not be able to keep pace with us, in which case we shall gladly gift you with our powers. It is also only fair to add that no humans are wanted for their supposed crimes more than we are. The arts of concealment are ours to bestow."

Edwin intercepted his Brethren. "If your casual slaughter of my free-roaming garden-beasts is anything to judge by, then Noah's Ark will be well and truly empty by nightfall at the end of this Millennium – empty of all humans as well as animals. Kill that I or We may live, is your guiding precept. Would that I had a killer's constitution, but I cannot quarrel with your precept. The self-willed can only cohabit up to a point. Each of us is too proud of his or her imperfections to tolerate any community for long. And this is as it should be. My only regret is that animals cannot be avenged on their human tyrants as we can on ours. My intention was to multiply my animals to the point where that should become feasible. Now you have set my work back somewhat." "But your Brethren will go out and avenge animals on your behalf. That will more than repay you for our precautionary measures on entering the Borneo Jungle that is your Estate!" Syfert remonstrated. "If it were not for the superhuman capacities of your nameless companion, they should repay me by avenging my animals at YOUR expense," Edwin countered with a quietly venomous lethality. "Such are the follies and injustices of this world that we can only absolve ourselves from our accidental misdeeds by withholding our membership of a shared Species. That is the only path for the likes of us – as you well concede," Syfert concluded. "Now I put my question to you again. Who is ready to go out and wage Armageddon with a difference?"

"I'll join you," the Annihilator affirmed suddenly. "But my weapons will come with me. I shall carry enough explosive on my person to precipitate an Apocalypse unprophesied by any mere Biblical seer." "Ah – we have one convert to our faithless Religion, I see! You remind me of the Professor in Conrad's *The Secret Agent*. By wiring himself up with enough explosive to kill himself and countless others around him within a large radius, he ensured his lifelong protection from arrest. No-one in Authority ever dared to approach him. Is he the one you're modelling yourself on, Mr. Annihilator?" A tone of cynical challenge entered his voice. "No – I am far worse than he could ever have been, in or out of the pages of Fiction. Not only is my arsenal far more deadly, but my purpose transcends his altogether. He was waiting on his own extinction, whilst his minions did his dirty work for him. I shall go out with a bang only after I have long savoured the whimper of the world. In joining forces with you, I am extending a privilege in recognizing you as my equals. But I will insist on carving out my own spheres of influence in the world, bordering on your own. Let us be Gods in our own localities, if there can be no one God in the Universe of all localities." Syfert considered this for a moment, then replied. "I see you've relaxed your ultra solipsism a trifle. We didn't want to spoil your cue, friend. But maybe you're rare in acknowledging our peculiar pre-eminence, shall we say? I wouldn't know how you've lived before coming to rest in this decaying Palatial residence, but both No Name Now and I are as inured to rough living and the transience of the Dispossessed as a pair of alien pods spiriting from one celestial craft to another. We never settle in one place for very long, nowadays. We consume and advance, emancipate and delegate."

"Before I discovered Edwin's refuge, I used to travel the Land colonizing derelict buildings that no-one else wanted to go anywhere near, never mind live in or share with someone like me. I was the Emperor of the Squats, abandoning Communes for the peace and power of my own shade. Rough living holds no mysteries for me. I'm no Nineteenth Century Russian Nihilist with Aristocratic connections in London Salon-Society. I wouldn't have made polite conversation with Lord Arthur Savile. Nor would I have failed for the umpteenth time to assassinate the Czar. I embody the Avatar that left Nechayev rotting in jail, brooding in the night of nothingness for a century, then settling in my soul like a Charioteer of Chaos. I'll eat just about anything and sleep in any pit I happen to find myself in. Moving always suited me before I settled here. Inertia is death, friction life. I long to ANNIHILATE as I go, to erase everything I pass. I'll leave with you tomorrow morning – but do not be surprised if our paths separate at some later stage." Edwin sighed softly. His freak-friend was a Judas-goat.

"I would be more surprised if they didn't – " Syfert replied slyly, well satisfied with his enticement of probably the most destructive revolutionary on the planet – albeit only in theory, at this stage. He turned his attention next to almost certainly the most destructive reactionary, and not only in theory, on the planet, Dr. Plague. "And how about you, then? The reservoirs of England await the blessings of your pioneering bacilli, as an Aperitif before atrocity. Release your cultures into the food-chain, spread your plague like invisible locusts. We shall be immune to its effects, I'm sure – being the friends of filth and the devils of degradation. And if not, that which does not kill us will strengthen us, as Nietzsche would say. For we cannot die, any of us. Even in the grip of the most terrible disease, we are immortal. No Name Now assures us of this, do you not?" The long-silent One stirred ever so slightly. "Nothing that lives has ever not lived and can ever die. Mutation is the thread tying the living and the dead. All will survive as such. I will triumph." "So there was no Creation – you see! There is only the Continuum of Creation and Destruction, forever spawning life-forms, spinning them out and then sundering them in the vortices of the Infinite!" Syfert cried out in confirmation. "No Name Now is a small embodiment of the great Sea of Chaos. He is a God in miniature, affirming that there is no God nor Devil – and no single Cosmos neither, but infinitely many. And our own Greater Selves are growths from the eternal seeds of our Being, especially fostered by such great encounters as we are all having now."

"I think we have the General Idea now," Dr. Plague asserted with a heavy exhalation of toxically odorous breath. "But until I have studied in close detail the special features of his physiognomy, I am undecided about giving my assent to your claims on his behalf. As for your request, that I should join you on your murderous travels across England and doubtless further afield, nothing should amuse me more if it were not for the fact that I can hardly contrive to carry my Laboratory on my back like an overloaded tortoise! And in spite of my presence in this curiously uncollectivized Collective, I always work alone." These last words were spoken with such a chilling finality and intransigence, even Syfert was momentarily shaken. "If you agree to offer your invaluable services to our movement, then I am sure No Name Now will offer his live body to the service of Science – not that Science could ultimately explain him. But if a *quid pro quo* is called for, then I think he might well deign to steep to such scrutiny." "Science does not need to explain, when it has the power to destroy!" Dr. Plague thundered in response. "The sixty four thousand dollar question is whether Scientists are prepared to use their knowledge to simplify drastically that which otherwise can never ultimately be explained. I am rare amongst Scientists in answering this question in the affirmative. But you must be aware that I am as a result a marked man in the world at large. I was obliged to go to ground when I discovered Edwin's Estate, and it has since provided me with the nearest approximation to a perfect Base I could ever hope for in this God-obsessed country. It is not in my interests to depart this Base, when I can work my fool-proof magic from within its inscrutable confines to spread over the Land like hemlock from Hades itself. I decline your request."

Syfert recoiled from this rejection, pondered awhile and then hit upon a more radical compromise. "Very well, then – be the spider in the web, if you must. But it might aid your Scientific understanding of No Name Now, if he were to demonstrate to you something of his true power. Are you willing, and ready, to be astounded in a way that even you have never been before? If so, then you may well feel that such is the cosmic protection he can offer you, that you can go about your deadly business anywhere in the world with absolute impunity. No Police or Security Force could touch you, Man! How about that, then? Can you bear to be unacknowledged for another single day? Can you also bear the spectacle of a superior Being in your midst?" Syfert risked eyeballing the megaton-megalomaniac in a perilous gesture of oneupmanship. "Well – can you, Bacillus-freak?" An atmosphere of chilling violence descended upon the Table, as the two antagonists summoned their utmost powers of will and devastation. Physical confrontations were rare in Edwin's Household, eclipsed as they were by the finer intensity of verbal, intellectual and psychological confrontations. But the churning stews of visceral hatred were never far from the surface of the proceedings. Though it was generally understood that a relapse into physical violence involved a lessening or breaking off of inner tensions and animosities. However, such was the capacity for Titanic rage among most of those assembled, that little of the interior of the Building would survive intact if a sudden outburst were granted free and prolonged rein. So a mood of concentrated control and restraint prevailed, as in a circle of Samurai contemplating realms that incorporated, yet transcended the merely martial spirit.

Edwin's Messianic placidity usually held sway when a war of words threatened to spill suddenly into a near-mortal clash of hands and feet, elbows and knees, heads, teeth and claws, and any available weapons from knives and glasses to chairs and statues and boiling liquids. But a shiver of panic ran across his death-pate visage whenever Dr. Plague or the Annihilator began to fume with livid temper. The others he could pacify as a rule. The slow volcanic eruption of Dr. Plague's ire was a truly mesmerizing sight to behold. Some chemical chain-reaction seemed to galvanize the toxic tone of his facial skin into a heated soup of fermentation, like an earthquake breaking up his rocky flesh in a flood of plasma. His poison-addiction was such that he could induce a chemico-physical metamorphosis in himself at will, like an irradiated Vulcan forging furies. His eyes became streaked with the burning blood of his long-cooked insides, as he focused all of his historic enmity in a single stare of feral, lycanthropic ferocity. He had distrusted Syfert from the very outset, suspecting him of having an Agenda of wrecking sabotage unacceptable to everyone in the house – except the Annihilator of course, but HE was the craziest free radical outside the bloodstream of Homo Sapiens he'd ever encountered! Like aberrant sub-atomic particles, all free radicals should be dragooned into an army of super-viral invaders. But Syfert was a strange one – black enough to be a fellow-spirit, but too damned elusive to pinpoint within a precise category. And he scorned Science, the fool! If he wanted a show-down with Dr. Plague, then by Satan he would have one!

The Great Buddha of bio-degradation rose slowly from his seat to challenge Syfert more directly. The distance between them was approximately six feet across the mighty Table and he would have had a long walk round either end of it. It seemed as if he could have spun the Table away into a corner of the room with no more than a flick of forefinger and thumb, or shattered it with a crashing fist, or simply dissolved it with the sheer force of his incurably diseased and deranged mind. His professorial frame suddenly shook with a strength that wholly belied its apparent reserves, like a sedentary blob electrified with monstrous energies. Syfert would have been almost as terrified of Dr. Plague as he had been of No Name Now when he first encountered HIM. But he was no longer timid, being cursed with the rapid fire of newly wrought sinews. He reckoned he wouldn't be needing No Name Now's intervention or protection on this occasion. For several moments they locked into each other's gaze across the Table-Top, like a pair of magnets resisting their final pull into the ring-furnace. Before either of them moved, Edwin raised his thin, gaunt frame up to its full height and pleaded for peace. "Aim your furies at the Heavens, by all means – but leave my menagerie intact, I implore you!" An incongruous streak of propriety crept into the faces of the two antagonists, as if some talking ghost had momentarily distracted them from their savage opposition. No sooner had Edwin resumed his seat, than No Name Now rose up from his, his legs powering him like automaton-shafts. A fearsome hush fell on the Assembly, cutting through the vector-beam that oscillated almost visibly – if not audibly – between the rival pair of eyes.

"You require a demonstration of my powers?" he addressed Dr. Plague, an eerie calm seeping through his speech. The latter was by now speechless with imploding rage, the trajectory of his animus spun out of its orbit by the sudden shift in the balance of forces prevailing at the epicentre of Edwin's kingdom. No Name Now did not wait for an answer, but resolved to silence his principle doubter – and the rest – at one swift stroke. "The lightning you are struggling to release shoots in an instant from MY fingers. Behold." So saying, he shot out his hand in the direction of Dr. Plague, his pulpy, hideously formed fingers stopping a few inches short of the latter's face. In the same bizarre interval of time a phosphoresent snake of light flowed hallucinogenically through the tips, stealing into Dr. Plague's toxin-armoured anatomy where it vanished completely for a few seconds. Dr. Plague smiled like a man-monster, convinced he had absorbed and neutralized a possible mortal threat, only to reassert his superior strength. But then his smile changed into an expression of apprehension, followed by fear, followed by panic, as his entire body began to vibrate and shake more and more violently. Then his flesh started to turn red, redder and redder still – until steam began to rise off him, along with great waves of heat felt by the others near him that raised the temperature in the room. A slow scream issued forth from inside his boiling belly and out through his spastic mouth, convulsing in a frantic rhythm with every other part of his anatomy. He started to expand and bloat like a blood-filled balloon, the fixed might of his stare cracking his skin.

No Name Now had the power to reverse in an instant the controlled devastation he was wreaking in this Connoisseur of chemical extinction. But a swift executioner's nod from Syfert impelled him on to a final conclusion. Everyone else, even the Annihilator, was hypnotically riveted by the literally incredible scene unfolding before them. Surely the Exterminator himself could not be exterminated? What should become of his Project? Who could continue it in his absence? These questions hung in the putrid air of their minds for a few more moments. And then Dr. Plague's scream suddenly became swallowed up in the terminal wheeze of his accelerated bodily expansion. His feet almost lifted off the ground as his torso burst through his clothes and his head acquired the proportions of an elephantine Billy Bunter. Finally, an explosive puff sounded and his entire physiognomy was obliterated from the inside out, like a handgrenade going off in a pomegranate or a mutant Mr. Creosote getting his (un)just deserts! The remains of the 'food' were spattered with his blood and entrails, as were the clothes and faces of many of those assembled. Even the nearest wall received a liberal coating of contaminated viscera. Nothing remained of the self-appointed Angel of Death but his scattered insides. He who lives by, etc.. The mysterious visitors had now established their ascendancy in the most emphatic manner possible. The stunned silence ensuing was longer and graver than any previously known under Edwin's precarious Hegemony. None of the Brethren knew quite how to respond to this total decimation of a Master of Evil as much admired as he was feared.

Edwin hung his head on his chest, an extraordinary air of resignation in failure weighing him down. Dr. Plague had held the hope of his Dystopian dreams, being the very same autonomous instrument of destruction for him as No Name Now so evidently was for Syfert. Except Dr. Plague had always had to work at his miracles of malevolence, whereas they appeared to spring like spontaneous fountains from the inhuman source lying at the heart of the Unnamed One. Even the Annihilator remained stuck for speech, if only a sardonic aside dismissing his old rival in the manner of James Bond over the spectacular death of a villain. He had lots of guts, etc.. But before everyone had had time to gage their shock more fully, oblivious of their bloodied faces, the Diabolical duo assumed complete control with a mesmerizing injunction that they clean the room by licking up every last trace of the bodily fluids of their erstwhile resident Exterminator. Syfert had had to undergo the same initiation into Malthusian cannibal Economics while eating the Oxfordshire farmer in a werewolf fugue spell ending his older incarnation. If one left no mess behind, one turned Habeas Corpus on its officious head! And what a potent efficacy must persist in the still warm quick of Dr. Plague's effluence! To finger the freshly spilt blood of violent criminals like Baby-faced Nelson used to be regarded as a method of re-invigorating the spirit, a sort of lapsed Pagan rite. How much more invigorating must be the consumption of such blood, especially irradiated blood? The immortality of the Grotesque was thereby conferred.

In face of the blank bewilderment of Edwin and his Brethren, Syfert responded thus: "Let us show you the way in this ancient Tribal custom, still practised in Borneo and other far-flung regions of the world – not to mention nowadays the dear old English Home-Counties!" The Annihilator was the first to manage a laugh at this, soon followed by Obscurius, Elethea and others.

Eventually, only Edwin remained silent – his face a canvas of aetherial Gravitas. Meanwhile, Syfert and No Name Now systematically gobbled up rather more than their fair share of the well-spread Smorgasbord that was Dr. Plague, and showing no ill-effects whatsoever tempted those onlookers in whom the lust for the extreme knew few bounds to follow suit. After all, one should experience everything in Life at least once – save nepotism and belonging to a golf-club. While the Annihilator saw it as a self-imposed duty in overcoming one of the last remaining obstacles to absolute license, Obscurius saw it as the ultimate sacrifice of Literature in the realm of morbidity. The women saw it as a decisive act of vengeance upon male power, a triumph over mere symbolism. Only Aleph and Solarius held out with Edwin against this seamiest of all descents from their craggy pinnacles of abstract purity into the Stygian morass of swallowed dregs. For the sake of sparing the gentler fanatics in their midst, Syfert and No Name Now proffered grace of abstinence to this disgusted Trio in the Castle of Cannibals. The others settled about overcoming the Taboo-fuelled organic resistance to partaking of one of their own kind, and on already full stomachs moreover. But they all needed one final test of their meta-humanity as Syfert would say, before going out and claiming the world by conquest. And what better sustenance could they crave than the divided chemical cake of Dr. Plague's indestructible residues?

No Name Now gave each of the consumers in turn the full benefit of a macabre energized blessing, while they rendered the room as spotless as a left-over plate licked by a ravenous dog. They all felt strangely fortified by this deed that placed them more firmly beyond the pale of Human Civilization than they had ever been before. And Satan alone knows how far removed they had always been from so-called normal social contact! Being born under ill-fated stars, no doubt – if there be any truth in this notion – they had grown up increasingly estranged from everybody and everything around them and beyond. Then they had fallen under Edwin's greater distancing spell, hardening their solipsistic obsessions beneath his roof. And now they had been inducted further still –

furthest of all – into the unsurpassable maleficence of their new astral governors and guides. Except that the freedom presaged by this induction was to prove yet more terrible than any governance they could conceive of. The burden they had all shared in quite independently of one another, having been relieved by the stimulus of their collective solitude – their Hermetic privation – would now intensify more than previously in a new cycle of exposure to the pursuit of the world, and then ultimately in their accountability to the Absolute itself, whatever that is. Edwin's spell – never once encumbering – was now broken, and most of his Brethren would shortly desert his crumbling refuge, leaving him a haunted immortal, a spirit-vampire starved of their invisible food. They thought they were soon embarking on the route to a vaster, self-ordaining Destiny. But they could not have known what truly lay in store. Their arrogance was blind.

Edwin never spoke again before retiring to his upstairs chamber, his face an inexpressible icon of the deepest wound a soul can sustain. Solarius and Aleph did likewise, departing like the dying retinue of an abandoned Sanatorium. Only the animals would keep them company from tomorrow. The core-colony of the movement towards a new Race of Outcasts stayed downstairs, doing a danse macabre well into the early hours, hurling plates around the dining-room and the Great Hall in a manner that would put Tristan Tzara and his feuding Dadaists utterly to shame. Eventually they collapsed into sleep on chairs and sofas or else the floor. No Name Now and Syfert didn't require much sleep, each one restoring himself briefly whilst the other looked on. Eternal consciousness without sleep would be a lot more unendurable than the prospect of eternal extinction without memory, for most living beings reconciled to the fact of death. But the thirst for immortality satisfied in No Name Now, and still raging in Syfert, inured them to the existential echoes of the self-conscious reflex – the time-honoured tedium vitae. Actually, nothing appeared absurd when everything stood ready to be eclipsed. The emptiness or surdness of existence posed the deepest challenge of all for negating minds craving revelation beyond bounds that must be broken. But there's always point in engaging this challenge. It is never meaningless.

Being awake, the night was at their mercy, held in the grip of their eyes, cushioning the dreaming bodies before them in razor-fine velvet. It might be the moment for a disappearance as mysterious as their original appearance, or else the moment for yet another massacre. But instead it was the moment for the conscious implantation of their mental seeds in the unconsciousness of the sleepers. Infusing elemental layers and strata of their Being with templates of terror, they fortified their innermost link with the fabric of externality. Their worst ambitions were already realized in the necessity of their potential. No ritual was required, no ten-year training or bowing to Gurus. The Process was the Result and the Result was instantaneous, easing out sans effort or sacrifice. A gift of license undermined the claiming of rights and performance of duties without a calculus of utility. Supernature didn't need to be moral, any more than nature – save the latter had paid too heavy a price on Bacon's rack. Supernature had no interest in being moral, only in being free of the constraints of nature and society, with the power to destroy and create. That was all that Life and Death at their best consisted of. But the Agents of this Continuum were henceforth to be all those denied their Birth-grace by Hierarchy's placemen, the reigning thieves of Selves.

The dawn came and was drunk in as visual blood. The sleepers awoke, rising out of their dreams like zombies refreshed. The significance of this day was too intense to grasp – the day the Grotesques came out of hiding to dazzle Humanity with their darkness. They would take with them only a few of their most treasured/accursed possessions, their ultimate keys to the Meta-Apocalypse. The rest could be left behind in the separated time-capsules confined to each chamber of Edwin's Kingdom. The Annihilator would take his chain-mail of cataclysms, Obscurius his rotting Opus, Elethea her witches' potions, Antarctica a sealed jar of ammonium, etc. Before Edwin appeared with Aleph and Solarius in tow to make his final plea, Syfert and No Name Now departed briefly with the Annihilator to investigate the contents of

Dr. Plague's Laboratory. "Is it booby-trapped?" Syfert asked the Annihilator. "Not with explosives – they're my speciality. He never believed in them. And I'm sure he had no time for such antics as putting chemical jars above his door. Quite frankly, he didn't think it necessary to secure his Laboratory, because he knew it was held in such awe by everyone else in the house – or virtually everyone – that he could dispense even with locks and keys. No-one dared venture in here, for fear of being contaminated. But I am not afraid of contamination, so I have seen inside once. It may not blow OUR minds, but it WOULD blow the mind of any half-way normal human being. I do assure you of that. We were enemies. But in one respect we were the same. We were absolutely resolved to be CHANGED by our chosen methods. And so his death was for him only another beginning in his perpetual vocation. His core-essence will have re-formed since you blew his anatomy apart – consider that. Meanwhile, crossing the threshold of his domain holds no fears for us, I trust?" He gazed steadily at Syfert as he tried the door-handle.

The door opened slowly into a darkened space surrounding a cubicle of pale light in the centre of the room. The Annihilator switched on the light, Dr. Plague having fitted his own electrics in Edwin's oil-fuelled mansion – to reveal a perfectly sealed chamber within a chamber. On the outside there was a veritable mountain-range of antique clutter and refuse, books, clothes, gadgets, mementoes, photos, figurines, rations, etc. But inside the Laboratory, all was was pristine order, clinical tidiness and surgical hygiene. Not an item looked out of place, every instrument and container having its precise function in an overall design of the most concentrated lethality. As they moved towards the sinister sanctum, they observed the diaphanous plastic sheeting glued to the floor with a firmly zipped 'doorway' on one side. It was about fifteen cubic feet in volume and a good five feet from the high Jacobean ceiling. The Annihilator pointed out some wrapped protective clothing beneath the work bench in the central space. "That was specially issued to him at Porton Down, when he researched there years ago. He stole it along with other materials which he brought here with him in a huge, customized van that he used to scour the countryside looking for a hide-out and a base. For the last two years he hadn't been wearing the clothing. He also stole enough raw materials to spawn his own viral and bacterial cultures, as you can see. There is enough material inside that cuboid den to wipe out the whole of Humanity several times over, if it could be released on a sufficient scale. His idea was to use birds like carrier-pigeons with tiny capsules of anthrax or ebola or whatever attached to their legs, and inside the capsules the viruses or bacteria would be admixed with acid. The capsules would then slowly corrode, thereby releasing the deadly concoctions over a very wide area indeed." "Does Edwin keep a colony of birds as well as animals?" Syfert enquired with an air of quizzical savagery. "Oh, yes – he has an Aviary in one corner of his Estate, where literally thousands of birds of every description can be bred. He had long ago entrusted it to Dr. Plague for his purposes. Before you two arrived on the scene, he was very near to completing his Project. But now that he's dead – if only in one incarnation – we can steal our opportunity to sabotage his work for our own ends. Yes?" An expression of radiant evil illuminated his face. Syfert reciprocated, while No Name Now looked on in silence, the unimpressionable face of the future. "As the saying goes – there's more than one way to skin a cat. And this way looks more effective than most." The two men chuckled, the electricity of their shared wavelength crackling quietly beneath their sounds. Syfert then frowned, a sudden thought striking him. "It's just occurred to me that the substances Dr. Plague exposed himself to in this see-through tent of his must have leaked out into the room and the rest of the house – and further still. Each time he entered and exited the zipped doorway, there would have been a toxic release, however small. So we must all be contaminated already." The Annihilator viewed him with a lofty smile. "You've got it in one, friend. Join the Club Mutant!" Syfert reeled momentarily, then just as swiftly recovered his usual macabre composure. "That won't set me back much. I've been devoting most of my vexed stay on this wretched planet to metamorphosis. I'll welcome a fresh challenge.

As for No Name Now, he could drink gallons of the stuff and scarcely notice the effects. He's the worst living Biological weapon on Earth."

Still the quiet monster kept his own counsel. "Having seen him despatch Dr. Plague, I'm willing – albeit reluctantly – to concede that. But with this arsenal at his and our disposal, he won't even break sweat in his electric war with the world – ditto for my explosive war and your occult war." "Mere electricity is the least of No Name Now's powers. But I am puzzled as to why Dr. Plague bothered with this elaborate cubicle, if it couldn't contain the toxins in any case. Was he working on a substance of such deadliness that it could only be introduced into the atmosphere by very slow degrees, in which case the people here would have time to develop an immunity to what otherwise might kill them instantly?" "Precisely that. Though he was also so obsessed with regimentation, that he needed at least one space to himself in this household in which he could create a microcosm of the world he sought to create in macrocosm. Here he could be the ultra-disciplined Elitist set wholly apart from 'the great botched and bungled' of the Nietzschean 'herd'. His most intimate Project was to create a compound that only targeted the genetic personality-types he hated, leaving others safe – and especially others of his type fortified in a peculiar way. Paradoxically, our contamination is protecting us against the world and in no way weakening us in our struggles against the great disease of Society itself. Let us step inside his domain and have a closer look at his works." So saying, the Annihilator tore open the zipped doorway, releasing more evils from the Pandora's Box of warped Science.

Stepping inside, the atmosphere seemed to alter quite perceptibly, a clinical coldness hanging like blades of ice. Lamps were positioned directly above the workbench, which supported numerous capsule-trays, sealed jars and bacilli, all labelled precisely. Under rounded lids on flat bases lay seed-beds that sprouted strange-looking cultures. Tables of contents sat nearby, along with precision-instruments, miniature spatulas, syringes and calibrated measuring-rods. A large Windows Computer sat on a side-table, and on shelves alongside one 'wall' were numerous journals, pamphlets and texts. Alongside one other 'wall' was a large cabinet of curiosities, including anatomical specimens in various states of morbid decay in jars of formaldehyde and pickle, and stacks of opaque containers of differing sizes and shapes. "Those contain his completed arsenal," the Annihilator remarked, pointing to the latter. "The remainder on the bench are still in preparation. He had everything from Botulism to Sarin in here, and some special compounds of his own we don't even have names for. Some of the materials he was able to order over the Internet. The anatomical specimens he used to test minute quantities of his preparations. There can be little doubt as to their effectiveness, although only dispensable animals from Edwin's Estate were used for the purpose. Humans will succumb no less spectacularly."

"I'm very impressed by the intensity and quality of his hate. He needed no justification for setting out to destroy Humanity. The sheer offensive banality of the great obstacle of massmankind presented him with a sufficient spur to extermination. I'm almost regretting having given No Name Now the signal to kill him. But I think his opposition to us would have necessitated it sooner or later. Do you know which containers contain what, in what quantities and concentrations? The ones on the shelves don't appear to be labelled like the ones on the bench. Presumably that's to keep his enemies guessing. Only we three are bold enough to investigate the contents, I'll wager. I was cursed with supernatural strength some while ago now, and you were only last night when you ate our ingenious friend. It lends a new twist to the Holy Communion – eh?" "I only ever attended UNHOLY Communion, so I wouldn't even know. But any unobliging gift from a higher destructive power or source is welcome, even for a supremely arrogant bastard like me." He removed from one of the shelves a grey, cylindrical container with a tightly sealed cap, and held it up in front of Syfert and No Name Now. "My guess is that there's enough lethal material in just this one container to wipe out the entire population of England. Should we look inside?" "Actually, there may be no need. Why break such a nice-looking seal, when we shall only be using it at a later stage? Besides, No Name Now has X-ray vision – if I'm not mistaken. He will tell us what he can see if I ask him to." "You're not losing your nerve, surely?" the Annihilator quizzed him. "No. But we don't know how much of the contents we might lose, if we open them now. The crucial point about all these substances is how and where to release them, so as to MAXIMIZE their range of efficacy. A few pounds of Plutonium aren't going to do much good languishing on the floor of this room – are they? We'll take all this material with us when we go. For now, I've seen enough."

"If it is Plutonium, it won't spill or puff at all. Only liquid gases or powders do that. And they're in different containers. Whatever is in here is in solid, block form. Of that I'm certain, judging by the mode of containment, weight and feel. Anyhow, if you don't want to break the seal, then let our friend use his power of magic vision to enlighten us. If he has laser vision too, I'm sure he'll unleash a very interesting chemical reaction." "We're all composites of stardust," Syfert interjected, "but He still kindles the star-flame within him. That is the origin of the myth of the red-eyed monster – and the green-eyed too." "Very well. I await his Demonic intervention with baited breath." No Name Now then began to focus intently on the container, his vision slipping out of its habitual register into another one altogether. No sparks flew, but after some while he spoke of a blue substance coated in grey, with a velvety crystal consistency. "That sounds like Plutonium," Syfert averred. "So how did Dr. Plague get hold of that in addition to the Chemical and Biological materials?" "He didn't. He never worked in a nuclear power installation. But he knew enough Physics to know how to produce it with the base elements, which he stole from laboratories. It was this material that he was consuming over a two year period, gradually building up his resistance like Rasputin with arsenic. If he had lived, it would have been interesting to see if he could have prevented the slow decay unto death. I think he had unlocked the key to that breakthrough within himself."

"Maybe. But it's academic now. If you want instant immunity

to this substance, let No Name Now instil it with a charism of stellar breath. I am willing to inure myself to this stuff." "Good," The Annihilator intoned. "Whether I outlast the Apocalypse in my present incarnation doesn't concern me. I SHALL outlast it in some incarnation or other. Death will be my servant, not my master. And only its conquerors will be free. I hereby release us into uncharted terrain." So saying, he broke the seal and plunged his hand into the blue death awaiting him, plucking out a sizeable chunk and holding it aloft before the others. Syfert then followed suit and handed the capsule to No Name Now, who fixed both of them with an omnipotent stare as he took out a huge quantity and without any further ado proceeded to swallow the lot. His stare signalled irresistibly that his Example should be followed, which it was. No immediate ill-effects ensued. But a Fate was thereby laid down, set in store – reversible only in the forge of a greater Power still, that of insuperable Will. The act performed, the seal was replaced and the three of them gathered up as many of the containers as they could carry to be transferred to a rusting vehicle of Apocalyptic transportation in lieu of the Four Horsemen arriving at Edwin's door.

Having awoken the stolen Brethren to command a silent nocturnal vanishing, they were surprised suddenly by Edwin's appearance, descending the Grand Staircase with Aleph and Solarius following behind in some macabre mystical Procession of a far from Holy Trinity. "I often rise at this hour to commune with the Dark that is closest to Dawn," he cautioned them. "Though on this occasion I have come to make a final plea with my loyal companions here. Surely the Transfigurations you all seek are attainable within the seamless boundaries of my Kingdom. Do not desert your only spiritual home for the warring desert of the degraded world. You are chasing the chimaerae of the Life of Action. Aspire again to the higher and nobler Life of Contemplation, in which your Visions are Sovereign. I impose no Rule here, as you well know. I offer you the freest retreat you could ever hope to find anywhere on Earth. Is this not a final resting-place for the Body and Soul and a launching-pad for the Mind and Spirit? I have so valued your presence here in my otherwise solitary, ghost-haunted eyrie, that your precipitate departure – maybe forever – feels to me in a very strange way like the loss of offspring. You are like the children I never had, albeit some of you are of my generation or even older. I know I cannot – and must not – prevent you from realizing your ambitions, if they of necessity embrace the conquest of other kingdoms. But hear the sadness in the heart of a peerless prophet knowing that he will shortly be devoid of his Brethren – the speeches and the silences, the clashes and the harmonies, the delvings and the atmospheres! Solitude is first nature to me, but how I have grown to relish the ungraspable animation of company! Leave me if you will. But I bid you to return if the world is impervious to your terror, or drives you back upon yourselves in the Wilderness exceeding all endurance. I fancy this House will survive the End of the World if it occurs, like the Biblical House of many Mansions. Yet my House contains Infinity without God. The Void fills with the endless reveries of intoxicated Egos. The Outcast is King. I implore you to honour Dr. Plague by waging war from a still centre."

"We'll bring you the head of the False Leviathan!" Syfert answered, resolved not to be swayed by this last reserve of rhetoric from Edwin. "You will do a profound disservice to Abstraction by serving Illusion!" Aleph concluded with a premise. "The Sun will draw you into the shadows of its heat, if you depart the light of this House," Solarius added gnomically. "We shall steal spots from the Sun and deliver them into your hands, illusion or no illusion!" the Annihilator proclaimed. The efforts of the Elders had clearly been to no avail. They resigned themselves to the prospect of a slow aetherializing out of existence, an invisible mutation into undiscovered corpses rotted with radiation. The House would fall like the House of Usher eventually, some stray tramp dropping a match in the undergrowth. Nobody would ever approach the charcoal carcass for fear of an occult contamination worse even than the nuclear kind. As it was, there had been no deliveries from the faithful old family-suppliers for a month at least. Soon they would stay away altogether, leaving the ageing trio to the self-sufficiency of vegetation sans vegetables.

The Brethren left Edwin silent on the staircase, swarming into the dark, thick morass of the Gardens to force their greedy passage to the boundaries, where they would let themselves loose upon the pastures and conurbations of England, psychically threaded through No Name Now and Syfert, yet granted all the leeway of Satanic Rottweilers on rice-paper leashes. They were already gifted with the subtleties and strengths of supernatural survivors on the horizonless battlefields of Cosmos and Chaos. The infiltration of a whole Country – and far beyond – was now going to be accelerated immeasurably. The Millennium was not far off now. The year was 1999, season indeterminate – like all English seasons for many a year. A war was being waged in Yugoslavia. But it would pale into total and utter insignificance, compared to the only genuine, necessary and desirable War that was shortly to be unleashed like a myriad of Yugoslavias across the entirety of the Planet. No Revolution in History could equal it.

TEN

The Annihilator led the anarchic army of powerfully deranged and slowly deforming supernatural freaks through the rich Plutonic foliage of collapsing structures, with its sudden, savage animal surprises swiftly curtailed by the Unnamed One, until a wide expanse of grassy scrubland opened up, revealing a vast, caged structure in the distance. "That's the Aviary I mentioned – and nearby is an abandoned fleet of vehicles which we can commandeer, for the time being at least," he remarked. "Hasn't it attracted suspicious attention from locals, not to mention the Police?" Syfert enquired. "In the past, yes. But as with the rest of Edwin's Estate and his now truncated Brethren, as long as there weren't any outward signs of subversive activity – and there never have been – the presumption grew that we were just a bunch of harmless eccentrics, like a Vegan Commune! And the Village Bobbies on their bicycles had no wish to negotiate the undergrowth unless they had very compelling grounds for doing so. As a result, we've been left alone. Even the spooks have steered clear, there having been no clear intelligence on Dr. Plague's whereabouts for years. As for me, no-one ever had any intelligence on me because I've never joined the Establishment in my life. And Edwin is seen around here as like another Marquess of Bath, who never goes out! Just look at THAT, against the dawn-light – a cathedral in metal! And THERE are our mobile homes for the next few days, weeks, months, years – who knows?!" The Aviary resembled a roller-coaster close up, or some unclassifiable sculpture slowly built up over decades by a lunatic genius and bequeathed to an ineffably mysterious posterity. The colony of birds inside it was dormant at this hour, but began to stir in unison as the articulate aliens approached. Soon a chorus rose up like an acoustic crest on the tidal air-waves, resonating over the Landscape for miles around.

"That can't be music for the neighbours' ears," Syfert commented acerbically. "I can't recall the last time they did that," the Annihilator replied. "It must be the call of the wild – the song of fellow-spirits hearing our footsteps." He then turned his attention to the fleet of single-decker vans and coaches – covered in black and red paint for the most part – lined up at one side of the Aviary. "Ah! Black and red – just the right colours for our ultra-anarchic assembly!" he declaimed in voluminous defiance of the birdsong. "Yes – a nice Stendhalian twist on the usual Aquarian yellow and green displays," Syfert rejoined. "And there are no crude symbols of the letter A in a circle sort to give the game away – and above all no CND signs, which would be a bit rich considering what we've just had for breakfast!" The Annihilator let loose a sick stream of ironic laughter. "But before we embark and depart, we must release the flock and grant them the savage freedom they've been craving for so long!" So saying, he took some keys out of one of his many labyrinthine pockets concealing Satan knew how many mined materials and stepped toward the great door that had always spelt confinement for the thousands of carefully nurtured and primed avian inmates. With two twists he unlocked it and then slowly pulled it open single-handedly, emitting an uncanny, imitative cry, as though he were possessed of the vocal chords of some pre-historic raptor. Within seconds the birds had alighted from their perches and flown out through the sudden inviting space, amassing a huge swarm that temporarily blacked out the nascent dawn-light.

As everyone stood rooted to the spot, their eyes fixed on the spectacle of the locust-like exodus to far-off lands, the Annihilator broke their sudden silence by exclaiming "Every single one of those birds, from the ravens to the starlings, is carrying sufficient lethal material to wipe out the population of a city – the end-game of Dr. Plague's patient plotting. And to think they were seen as no more than the hobby of an innocent recluse! Well, the world is now moving into its countdown phase!

Throughout the world, in Europe, Africa, Asia, America, EVERYWHERE, people are going to be dropping, gasping, writhing, flaking, churning – dying in the most agonizing throes imaginable! And only the most truly abominable Outcasts such as ourselves will survive to form the new licentious Dystopia! All the crises in the World are going to be eclipsed very soon, friends. And in the meantime we shall sweep up our straggling enemies in the wake of our Hermetic messengers of Pestilence! The impurest purification of the Species is at hand! Let us take to the roads of this tottering Civilization in our untouchable convoys and aim our most potent venom at its very heart and nerve-centre – the Capital of this wretched Country no less, LONDON!" Henry the Fifth at Agincourt could scarcely have aroused a more enamoured response from his listeners – only THEY were aiming their venom-tipped arrows at the henchmen of England's greatest historic foe and were all uniformed lackeys to a man.

The manned fleet of vehicles departed from Edwin's Estate unseen and unheard by the still-sleeping denizens of an unchanged rural idyll. Although the Landscape was bathed in a gentle morning light, the death of night darkened the omnipresent dew. The journey to the epicentre of world-trade in every commodity or enterprise trapped in Capitalism's clutches, the once-City of dreadful night now glittering in falsest light, advanced in the pattern of stalking serpents or feeding tentacles co-ordinated by a central brain. At a signal from the risen Anti-Christ shadow-cast- ing the moral universe, all the vehicles converged on an old manor-village on the outskirts of the Metropolis – a Tudor heart squeezed in a suburban skin. Here was the Base from which to launch the final assault upon fragile Power and Authority, the Fulchrum from which to lever the pivotal Planet-City into the visionary blackness of Post-Millennial aeons. It being the Sabbath and still early in the morning, the cosy little crofters' time-capsule had barely woken to the archaic rhythm of its daily rituals. The

Church-bells, calling the faithful to their knees, wouldn't break the sleepy silence with their stirring, mournful peals for quite a while as yet, and even the Pagan animals made no sound at this hour. All the inhabitants, each intimate with the others to the closer degrees, dreamt of bucolic idylls in their beds, their minds uninfiltrated by urban Media. They invariably rose with the presumption of a changeless provincial-rustic simplicity hanging in the air outside their windows. But this morning they would not rise, or if they did, they would step out into a seamlessly transformed space that would swallow their identities whole and deliver them into the Hereafter uprooted from the Earth and unburied with the Immortals. There'd be no Bobby to blow a whistle in the wind.

The buses converged upon the lone community from all points of the compass, meeting at its centre in the market-square, where a few rough sleepers prostrate on benches or in doorways shuffled slightly but slept on. The shopping-malls in these old habitats were nowadays magnet-arenas for the outlandish, the rural gangs and urban drifters. Alienation had seeped into the fabric of extended family, inserting black holes in the close-knit. The Outcast-Elect descended from the buses, espying their novel spirit-terrain. The rough sleepers were in an instant possessed of supernal breath, invigorating their greed. The village was powerless in their power, a horizontal web spun from the usurpers at its centre. No lengthy deliberations were needed. They instinctively knew what was to be done, what had already been done in such places all over the country, only with the inimitable signature of the Supreme Omen-Bearer himself. Spreading out in every direction, each one of them moved in total silence toward a self-targeted house, mentally pulverizing and devouring it as they entered the garden or alighted on the front steps, re-possessing the stone, brick, plaster or timber skeleton in the envisioned act of subtilizing its entrails. Each paused only to savour the imminent feast, salivating in the ether of his breath. Then with sudden, effortless rushes of unnatural strength, they quietly unhinged the doors and stole without shame across the thresholds of dozens of legitimate little private kingdoms, picturesque and still, haring like solid ghosts up rickety flights of stairs to behold the locked hearts of the bedrooms with their prostrate, unwitting occupants superstitiously protected by doors and rugs.

The latter were allowed no time to awaken and say their last prayers, as their uninvited fetchers claimed their flesh and gulped their viscera in swift blurs of frenzied massacre. The village was thus emptied of its population and as swiftly replaced by its secret destroyers, as the morning matured and no News travelled across the Land to alert unsuspecting visitors, not to mention Authorities. When a Nation is immersed in conflicts abroad and the preparations for a new destiny, it may not notice the most sinister cancer of all eating its passage invisibly from its boundaries to its core. Who in London knows what is happening at any given time in some remote rural village rarely frequented by strangers, miles from Civilization and so inbred no relations ever escape from it? Eh? And if the distance is then narrowed substantially, does it yield any difference in their awareness? No. This all-consuming transition is so seamless, it is perceptible only to One who sees with the Eye of God. And yet God, if he exists, is too absent from Earth to prevent what is happening. His Power is curtailed in a realm that carries Evil to a higher Power still. The New Settlers inhabit their Headquarters as an open Fort, probing the Peace deep beneath its surface. London is in a state of muted chaos, its facade of normal operations slipping gradually to reveal the spilt ferment of Millennial expectancy. In a world – and period – seemingly devoid of miracles, a feeling is growing among swelling pockets of the population that some great miracle MUST occur in the near future if Life is ever again going to be remotely worth living for most people.

But the miracle in question will not of course be of the conventional Religious kind, or indeed of a nature yet clearly imagined, let alone comprehended by the vast majority of Mankind, be they secure or dispossessed. It will be enough for them that just SOMETHING should happen that can tear their lives – if only for the one instant – out of the rigid joints where they are set in Society's rotting anatomy. Those who are not bound for Jerusalem or Mecca, but wait rather for some indigenous Saviour of London to emerge at the Twelfth Hour and ASTONISH them in a manner leaving Cocteau long dead, are counting the days like prisoners in their cells. They may embrace any of the Heinz 57 varieties of ludicrous cults flourishing like candyfloss conjured from charlatans' hands, but the underlying momentum toward the Unspeakable is far beyond their control. They are gathering their madness in readiness for an explosion of the deepest suppressed rage, that will inevitably leave them behind in its own wake. Joy does not enter into the equation, save for the moneyed and the superficial – the saccharine set. Being where the sun rises first on Day One of the New Millennium, with quintessential cocktails in their hands and cheesy images in their minds, followed by hours of exhaustive emoting, is all that concerns the latter. No calamity must be allowed to upset their frivolity, not war nor dark magic. But all these clowns prancing and prattling on Capitalism's sinking stage will soon hang in the Void – strung puppets with half-severed heads swinging in the bleakest winds of the Infinite.

The Millenarian sects in America, locked in confrontation with a pseudo-Democratic Republic, are spearheading the revolt of the disaffected masses in every country against the Plutocratic conspiracy of World-Govn't. In England the revolt is less militaristic, less fanatical, more anarchic. The common thread is the Apocalyptic Vision. But this thread is being given so many crazily inspired twists as to flower into a cornucopia of chaos. Revolution is in the air again, dancing on the grave of Ideology, feeding off the roots of Pagan renewal. Communism and Socialism are deservedly dead. Religion and Morality MUST die in a gasping duet with Capitalism and Statism. True Anarchy is about to be born – maybe for the first time ever in Human History, insurrecting from the swamps of Global Annihilation. Humanism has been only the prelude to the Beast. The Great Menu of Mediocrity that is Liberal Pluralism is being consumed in a savage swirl of Dialectical derangement. The rigor mortis of Coalition and Concensus is being unlocked by the electrons of the electorate, the free radicals in the Body-Politic. Academia totters on its pedestals of phoney Specialisms, before dropping headlong into the bloody slush of Populist sedition. In the kingdom of the Nobody, the Nihilist is king.

The Fin of each Siecle invariably throws up some fresh, cyclical wave of decadent froth. But the end of the Twentieth Century is far outstripping the passive, sickly Aesthetic of the Nineteenth Century, in its sheer swell of destructive potentialities. A fragile accord may have been struck in Yugoslavia, but the various dispossessed tribes of London have recently launched a day-long assault on the Square Mile itself – the greatest global citadel of financial power – staging riots reminiscent of those led by Lord Gordon over two centuries ago, in 1780, witnessed by the young William Blake, hungry for images of fiery Apocalypse. For six hours riot-police fought pitched battles with masked and painted warriors intent on besieging the besuited, wide-boy gamblers with the Nation's Capital in their towering, aluminium-plastic glass prisons. Finally, the revolting peasants of the post-post-pitchfork Age retreated to Trafalgar Square, where their fellow-precursors in 1381 had ended their own bloody affray, likewise the Poll-Tax rioters in 1990. (Indeed, the Peasants' Revolt of 1381 had been provoked specifically by one of the first impositions of a Poll-Tax in English History. Its Geographical locus has since evolved into a magnet of repercussive force.) So, the Stage was well and truly set for an Inspirer from without to galvanize these ravenous pillagers into an infinitely more potent still, and widespread Revolt, in time for and in tune with the greatest upheaval ever to erupt.

The omnipresence of the surveillance-camera would be of no more consequence than the statutory Bobby on the Beat, when sufficiently large numbers of supremely fortified freaks of (in)human nature laid terminal waste to the arbitrary old Meantime Centre of the long-navigated World. The apparently futile gesture of causing millions of pounds worth of damage, that would only be repaired in due course amid further tightening of already constrictive Security, would however this time around propel and combust a truly critical phase of sustained combat against so-called Civilization – culminating only in the eternal night of the

Human Species. The Ground was shaking – the Ground was prepared. No Name Now's Sovereign Assumption whispered itself in every breeze, blowing from nowhere apparent. The Annihilator's appetite was wetted, like a slow sharpening of knives in the Cosmic background. Syfert's black demon descended on every desert, gifting solitary wanderers with Enochian tongues of devastation. The split atoms of Dr. Plague re-assembled themselves in every corner of contamination across the Globe. Hereby the phoney Ethics of the City of London's Anti-Capitalist rioters would soon be trumped by the unequivocal embrace of Evil for its own superior sake. No opportunities would be lost in the remaining six months of History to consolidate the grown culture of murderous opposition to the Old/New World Order that was being screwed down in desperation like a fragile lid on a volcanic dome. Throughout every medium and channel, from the Street to the Internet and back again, incongruous alliances of otherwise conflicting groups of Pariahs beyond the pale were being formed, with a great clearing Vision of a Leap into some terrible Transcendence on the far side of the Millennium-Meltdown. Neo-Nazis buried the hatchet with Revolutionary Socialists, Anarchists and Nihilists; Survivalists, Supremacists and crazed Militia overlapped with hoboes, drifters and serial killers; while cultists, sub-cultists, Underworlders and Isolates merged into a malign unity.

Every weapon, from the anatomical via the mechanical to the chemical and biological, was being pressed into service by the Demi-gods of unleashed Democratic powers against the arsenals still held in the fractured hands of ruling Elites and crumbling Hierarchies. Even the Messianists now envisioned Christ as a wrathful Titan, unburied and re-awakening to petrify the Pharisees of Plutocracy in lifeless, immutable stone. Christ and the Anti-Christ were in truth and potentia One, awaiting their ultimate source in the all-comprehending shadow-embrace of the Nameless One himself. If the power of money and the hubris of authority could not be overthrown, or even seriously weakened by means of gesture-Politics, then they certainly could and would be by the Force Majeure of an almost unprecedented Revolution, almighty in its presumption of dethroning the Almighty. No other act or argument would suffice. The rights and wrongs of all issues were finally outweighed by the wild freedoms of Atomists of Supernature sublimely unconcerned with Nature, Species, History, Society and Order. The Reign of the Outcasts would not therefore be a reign as such, but rather a perpetual release from the greatest of all burdens inflicted by some members of a Race on other members. If Justice did not demand this victory, then the untrammelled spirit wrested by the truly Autonomous did demand it.

Another engine fuelling the flames in the Millennial-Apocalyptic cauldron was of course Prophesy. From the aforementioned Book of Revelations to Nostradamus, the pseudo-divination of the Future had evolved into a veritable Industry of preposterous Faith, no less thriving in the Post- than in the Pre-Rationalist Age. The absurdity of this whole phenomenon resides not only in the unthinking, impulsive tendency to embrace the most fanciful and far-fetched of superstitions – a defining characteristic, if there be one, of most if not all cults and sects – but also and above all else in the implicit denial of freedom lying at the very heart of Deterministic creeds which brook no deviations from their pre-Destinarian blueprints. This is the real affront to all TRUE Heretics – that the Future MUST always be as predictable as the Past is already known and controlled. For the true Heretic, Time is so elastic that absolutely nothing is or can be certain – not even the certainty of uncertainty itself. One can no more predict the Future than one can define the Present, and only the tyrants of the Species would ever want to do so. The highest free agents in each universe always have a remaining trick up their sleeves by which to confound and upset the manic programmers of Life. These Beings will accept the label of Heretic if the Orthodox put it on them, though they would rather adopt no label and stand aside from any such binding opposition. But the onus on the true Heretic is to rescue the Individual and his atomic freedom from the conspiracy of the Collective and the arbitrament of Authority.

Greatly exercising the minds of the many, as July 4th, 1999

approaches, is Nostradamus's supposed prediction that 'the King of Terror' will suddenly emerge from his lair and wreak such havoc and mayhem as to bring about the End of the World – rather a far cry from the cherished Object of American Independence Day, it would appear! The Four Horsemen of the Apocalypse – War, Death, Famine and Plague – will signal impending doom with thunderous hooves, ushering in 'Angolmois' or 'the Reign of Mars'. But what 'signs' are there portending this calamity? World War Three is surely not as imminent as this? An asteroid is unlikely to stray so soon off course. A swift upsurge in Global warming would be a welcome relief in this Land of perpetual winter! Conversely, an Ice Age seems equally improbable during such a short time-scale – though if the New Puritans are permitted to get their way, the resulting moral temperature-drop should well precipitate the necessary conditions! (In fact, the prediction rests on a simple linguistic error - diffrayer eliding into d'effrayer, kings not being noted for giving away money!) As for the 'Infinity Day' scenario, it would be a welcome variation on the alleged Millennium Bug buried deep in the Continuum of the computerized world! Such assininities bring a smile to the eyes and mouth of a Satanic sceptic, who knows full well that the energies of Irrationalism can be put to much darker, Cataclysmic uses. The smugness of Science and the Common-Sense of Society are perhaps even greater obstacles to the greatest emancipation of all than is the blindly atavistic idolatry of prophets.

Let the secret worshippers of the Anti-Christ congregate publicly before the cave-mouth of the Inferno to await their Profaner's Coming, while the loud Acolytes of Christ flock to Jerusalem to squat there like latter day St. Anthonies imploring their Saviour's blessings! They would all erase their Identities in the subsequent swell and clash of precipitating forces, yielding up the monstrous mirror-image of a Species transcending itself finally in unashamed savagery and awesome pre-possession. The legacies of creeds were nearing their necessary End, enslaving men's minds and souls for Millennia, only to light and combust the

Great Bonfire of Books that would purify the essence of Beings no longer moored to the dead sea-bed of History. Savanorola and the Nazis had a point — they just burnt the wrong books. Bibles and Manifestos were fit for the flames. However, works of rare perception and analysis — which laid down no Laws and revealed some shadowy outline of the Infinite — must always be hoarded and treasured against the well-oiled rubbish-piles awaiting the ignited fuse of severe judgment. Existence remained the stark cradle of Phantasy, confounding all Vision formed from the Word and not the Deed. No prophetic creed could transfigure Existence — ever. Only the most powerful and palpable manifestation of Supernature could achieve this, Nature corrupted to the highest Index. It may appear as the Light of the World to the benign Dispossessed, or else the Dark upon the face of the Void to the hell-bent Oppressed. But in truth, it is neither. It is rather a fissure, that spreads and swallows up the Moral Universe in its entirety. What it bequeathes on the far side of the Moral Universe is unimaginable to the Unknowing. The Earthly Instrument has always been sought and is now at hand, to deliver Humanity beyond Deliverance, to convey it past the Millennium to end all Millennia.

ELEVEN

The End of the World predictably never came on July 4th, the self-styled 'Kings of Terror' imploding impotently in basements and garrets up and down the Land – although the brief blacking out of successive regions of the Earth by the moon-obscured Sun on August 11th, while not bringing to every life-form terminal starvation of photosynthesis, would yet provide a cue for the truly awakened Kings of Terror to signal the Omen that would come more fully to pass at the End of the Year. In the meantime Syfert and Company laid low and incubated their heresies to an even greater degree than before, attracting no official scrutiny from outside the sleeping cocoon-village they had so radically and effortlessly purged of population. There is little point in giving this village a name – by the by, for the benefit of the putative Reader – since as of its re-population it has had no name to speak of. Suffice to say that its location is just outside the dud Magic Circle described by the M25, a precise leverage-point on a secret map of disruptive fulchra.

Visiting relatives and friends, passing strangers and drifters, even the odd tourist, finding a mysteriously altered yet quietly surviving place, disappeared with varying degrees of swiftness and alterior purpose while exploring too inquisitively for their mortal safety. Certain systems ground unalarmingly to a halt. There was no Station for a start, while the solitary Bus was not missed. The Post-Office and Bank were redundant museum-pieces in a Hermetically sealed local economy that had abandoned money.

Shops fell imperceptibly into decay and inertia, the basic necessities of food and clothing rendered monstrously contingent. The empty Estate Agent's Office still advertised Property, which no longer served any real purpose beside that of temporary, covert shelter for alien settlers who would instead gladly take their rest in the ether-groves of Outer Space. The Police-Station stood as a symbolic reminder of a former regime, in which rotund and beaming amateur cyclists went about their uneventful daily rounds of re-assuring vigils. The Mall was an empty Arena, filled with the ghosts of ragged Gladiators. The Village-Hall, previously a forum for flower-arrangers, was now an epicentre of universal Demonology. The Church had become an inversion of itself, a pitch-black edifice, a pentagram of forces. At some stage the local M.P. or a Chief Constable or a Magistrate would arrive in the Village, and finding nothing humanly familiar there, would raise the national alarm – unless of course they were fatally intercepted by feral apparitions, as had happened all too often elsewhere.

The assault on London would take effect like slow hemlock. The birds were doing their unwitting work in infinitessimal stages – as the crow flies, one could indeed say! And like the much more innocent swallows, their orbit ringed many a sea and far-off land. People would soon be dropping *en masse*, succumbing to unknown agents in the atmosphere. Satellites may record the trajectory of the plague-flock, yet not detect its issue. The survivors would be the toxic Essenes of the New Millennium. Only the Supernatural Few were cursed with the sinewy, fibrous strength to resist radiation-sickness, the tens of thousands optimally suited for the stewardship of the Planet in No Name Now's hidden remit. The Plutonium-Glow was already sketching its mercurial deposits in the flesh-pools and pits of the receptor-anatomies of Syfert's Company. The Annihilator's face was suffused with grey light, El Greco and Goya twinned in grotesque sublimity. His jagged, satyriacal features swelled with an added bestial power, the certainty of outliving mere death. Syfert's eyes shone like a warlock's. He was the Goat of Baphomet, a werewolf sprung from the Dog-Star. Obscurius had a new material with which to embalm the corpse of

Literature. The Pulsar of his rotting entrails timed the screed of Eternity. Elethea oozed vampiric lusts in a murky red flush of light. Antarctica frosted over livid secretions, her metabolism sinking into the deepest oceanic recesses. As for No Name Now, he remained the same. He could never resemble anything more horrendous or potent than himself. The toxin didn't so much wash off as disappear into him – absorbed like foul light into an impermeable black hole, a Venusian void.

None of those assembled missed Edwin particularly. His influence had been quietly electrifying in its own domain, but a markedly different aethos reigned in the present setting. No Name Now exuded an unchallengeable air, which however he never required to demonstrate in its physical form of manifestation. The others around him were like parts of himself sloughed off and re-ingested, notwithstanding the spaces in between. In spite of the superlative singularity of each part, it never occurred to any one part to separate more sharply from the spreaded totality. The Anathemata were split up and re-combined among the organs of an absolute Selfhood. The squatting Chimaera was strengthened by dismemberment, each head governing a body guided remotely from an invisible centre. No latter-day Bellerephon with his bow and arrow would know where to aim. The nerve centre had no fixed locus – it coalesced in at least four dimensions. The heart of Heresy displaced itself like the shadow of Hermes. And its message to Humanity was: You're going to get the Second Coming you deserve! You have – in part – summoned me, however unwittingly. And I shall have my hour – I shall shatter the glass of Eternity, embedding its shards in the great, swollen Body of Mankind! An infinity of inods will churn in the soup of a changed Cosmos, a vast quake of corpse-lava! Visions of ultimate Terror will be conjured up, the like of which were never seen, even by William Blake or the Marquis De Sade.

No Name Now stood over the nucleus of his people/mutants – a silent giant, shimmering greyly – observing from a distance of discreet influence the map of local destiny laid out and marked on a table-top in the middle of the living-room in the expropriated house. Syfert espied the lines of force radiating inwards from Green Belt boundaries along arteries of fire to the soft heart of London, as if he were looking into the map of his own brain or that of his greatest enemy more like. Streets were not simply routes for conveying vehicles from A to B, but the deliberate and haphazard Geography of the Psyche – the causeways and tracks of marchers and wanderers alike, the cooled prints of heated motions. He was searching for a pattern, a shape or form that should symbolize the fate of the City in the imminent energizing of its destruction. He saw it as an animal heart cut from the sockets of England, cable-threads protruding from the tangled pulp of sacs and valves. It could be squeezed and squashed in the mind – and hand – of an all-seeing and unseen visionary. The animal in question was not a lion but a jackal, a feral Satan swollen in the act of consuming the fat of the Land in the absence of predatory rivals. The jackal was expendable, an alibi for Apostates, going proxy for cherished Diaboli. It lay buried in an unconsecrated grave, its extracted and transplanted heart pumping blood through the living veins of Humanity's impostors, the alien ingestors of ruinous entrails. It was possessed and then re-possessed, the infinitely mortgageable carcass and blood-sump of the Hypertrophic sinden. Syfert was seeing the various Districts of the City inter-communicating and inter-locking like the chambers of the heart, feeding the perspective of the supersonic circumambulator. No man in only one District could quite see how it fitted with its neighbours in a hot shooting glance, without the map of the Totality etched eidetically upon his inner eye. Syfert pared this living image to dust, with Nelson's Column at its centre crushed straight down into its base.

The Annihilator, standing at his side, saw only the Semiology of rubble, the reddened lard of a population, the scorched residues of bodies silhouetted on stone. In the Rorschach Ink-blot of his blinding eye the integuments of the mapped City darkened to wisps of charcoal-ash delineating a whirlwind within a vortex of dead Gravity. The Houses of Parliament spun and sank into subterranea, vanishing in the vapours of their presumptuous Sovereign mystique. Obscurius, sprawling offensively over one side of the table, saw the fossil-traceries of Language's cancers grown from the soil into symbols. The broken and repeated trajectories of Life's foot-bound vessels wrote their stories into the composition of his irradiated Blood-Book, the all-consuming cake thrown in the face of Civilization. The women saw the relics of Roman Chauvinism, ordering Destiny in the Geometry of Patriarchy. Celtic Goddesses would always deviate from the straight road, even stripping the tarmac with their finger-nails off the long, winding lanes, which had sprung spontaneous from the womb of their whims. Boadicea was reborn in many shapes and forms – a Giantess with a barking voice ejecting enemies' souls into a perpetual Limbo, an Empire-eating cannibal immune to punitive poisons. In A.D. 61, London had been sacked by the said woman with her wild, warrior-tribe. So perhaps Elethea and Antarctica should steal the initiative from their male monster counterparts, and lead the next march on London with a conquering vengeance not seen since their Iceni forebear?

A strategy took shape amongst the feuding atoms of the non-putative Group-Mind – suggesting the need to place a single plague-bearer in every major, long-rotten Borough of the Great corrupt Metropolis of all Metropolises, so as to contaminate the Whole simultaneously in each part and then to constrict the Centre with applied pressure from the Peripheria, twisting a toxic tourniquet round the very neck of the Body-Politic itself. No Name Now envisioned scattered cells of fellow-Assassin-Acolytes in a non-Hashish inspired reverie, burrowing subsistent on the far sides of the City, merging with their ineluctable movement in accelerated steps of murderous mayhem. The River of Fire snaking through the forests of the City at Midnight at the End of the Millennium, would be extinguished by a velvetine garrotte of spiralling Gravity.

The 'Figure' of London has never truly been seen from the air, since all Aeronauts to date have lacked the Imagination of Astral Visionaries. The latter, in being grounded corporeally, must therefore strive for the 'Vision' that unfolds around every corner of the City, the streets of which are strung together with the rough pearls of a Mythopoetic narrative. Even the most inspired Maps serve only to freeze the contours for an unconventional Seer, refusing to be trapped in an alternate Time in which Space is re-arranged. There is no true substitute for the sudden, sublime unities of living Experience. The degraded Realism of the Map and the Print, the Chronicle and the Photograph, deprive the Place and its makers of the shapes of an elusive Essence. The image of Medusa, with her severed serpent-head, can readily appear before the eye of One seeking to repair the damage done by Perseus; to re-unite the Gorgon with the body of an alien land-mass, to resurrect a monstress of Myth in a time and place of other provenances. But then Paris and Rome and Athens et al could doubtless be configured in this guise, the cranial skeletons of their designs wreathed in shooting arteries of streets that stretch each point of the Human Compass. The Beast of the Apocalypse also had a fat head, though his Return will be pre-empted by the Satan of the Thames – that torpid gash flowing like a rictus across the face of a still half-hidden Ogre. The stars are in the River's silt and its silt is in the stars. Therein is the secret of things, that is no secret to the deep-seeing Eye.

The Bear and the Boar, the Cock and the Cat, the Fox and the Wolf, the Dog and the Rat, the Deer and the Bull – these were the animals of London, both within and beyond the pale of domestication, falling through the abysses of neglect onto the ancient flats and blood-beds where the Hunter forever pursues his prey and the Gaoler claims his prize. The residue-trails of death, destruction and decay trace through Time the lineaments and the Legacies of the yet undead, if long-travestied City. He who divines the forms of these trails acquires thereby the Power to obliterate and transmute the ossifying detritus of dull Architects' dreams – those Freemasons in a Temple of Post-Modernity, who have though no Religion posited above the dim prisons of their clay-sunk designs. The Figure rising from the swamps of Perception's Parallel issues neither from Design nor Accident, but rather from the ruptured harmony of symbolic forms. Chimaerae evaporate away to throw up an Archetype, a Protean entity super-imposing its image upon the Eye of receptive mind, gelling the City's Olympian observers.

When Syfert sees the bleeding Bull of London Lanes, it has all of the active terror of the Cretan Minotaur, its proportions gigantized by cannibal-feasts, its features fantasticized by cavernous entrapment. When the Annihilator sees the head of a Boar, it is the wild Caucasian Boar of untameable ferocity, roaming and crashing through a mirage of Middlesex Forest, forever uncaptured and never to be served up on some Monarch's silver platter. When Obscurius sees a red-eyed Rat, it is swollen with the sewage of centuries, its needle-teeth flashing brilliant-white in a Plutonic pall, scavenging off the Corpus of all sentimental Life. When Elethea sees a feral Cat, it is a stray freak from an old imported Menagerie, as wild as a starved Cerval yet as large as a sabre-toothed Tiger grown from reactivated genes. When Antartica sees a lone Bear, it is as white as a pearl-furnace, consumed with the stragglers of exploration, not dancing in chains on a tub to a master-piper's tune, no soft-bellied, brown-haired puppet of Man. And when No Name Now sees an animal of London appear before him – the potent Figure of the City – it is of course only Himself that he sees, reflected and revealed in a mirror-pool of darkened light. These Talismans cannot be placated, emerging from origins older than any Religion and more momentous than the latest Science. Technocrats are no match for Titans, Plutocrats for Plutonians, sub specie aeternitatis. Vision gives the Outcast his hand waging the War of the World.

The Solar Eclipse cast its slicing shadow across the Earth like a grey-blue portent of the shapelessness of things to come. Confusion more than chaos came to Cornwall, the Anarchists foiled by the weather and British Rail. And in the kingdom of dark glasses, the pin-hole camera was king.

The blackness of the sky was over-anticipated by the Satanic Insurgents, shunning the light on the Uplands beneath an Hegelian Sun. The odd idiot doubtless went blind, thus depriving Mankind of no great sources of perceptive illumination of matters arcane and diverse. Some German Entrepreneur, his goose-stepping finger on the commercial pulse, registered some supereffective Teutonic solar shield-prototype very cheaply, whereupon half the population of the New Model Army of the Greater United Germany obediently bought – only to be upset by a rain-forecast, which it transpired was not nearly as bad as predicted! But the Outcast-Elect stole yet more strength from the moon-starred Sun, while its Corona ringed the black orb of its transient sleeve-heart like a diamond-vice. When a Being descends from the invisible core of such a radiant ball of destructive fire and it sees through the vastly magnified intensity of its eclipsed light, it cannot be blinded visibly to the known, but only subtly shared secrets of Itself. Thus No Name Now sucked the Eclipse into his own Eye, sharpening the focus of his camera obscura hidden inside the imponderable psyche of a star-fiend sizing up human anatomies.

Deaths from mysterious or allegedly mysterious causes mysteriously increased, in places as far afield as Lincolnshire and Zanzibar. The birds had scattered, alighting here and there, mating and breeding, fructifying their toxin-seeds. Some died or got bagged on the wing by eager shots, spreading their sung or silent Gospel of contamination far beyond the grave of field and pot. The pun on the Millennium-Bug duly generated great fears of pandemic diseases, old, new and unimaginable – necrosing fascitis being a mere Aperitif before the great, fleshy Smorgasbord of bacterial meals at dear old Hugh Manity's expense, nodding askance at Flann o'Brien, that were yet to come. The common cold of course, as incurable as ever, accounted for astronomically larger numbers of deaths among the elderly and infirm than did for example the dreaded meningitis among the bright, fresh young hopes of Mankind. Millennial madness thus makes hypochondriacs out of even the most morbid masochists for whom death by electrocution would be a virgin-thrill on the threshold of an eternal Afterlife of chthonic tortures. There is then no juster cure for the phobias and allergies and phantom-plagues of the weak and credulous than an authentic black miracle of Globe-sweeping devastation, performed at the inscrutable whim of One Cthulhu or some such.

TWELVE

A time for splits is portended among the Supra-Nietzschean Knights of the rectangular Table, whereon the Map of unprecedented Doom is plotted on the externalized Grid of their magically aligned mind's eyes. No Name Now won't quite ride out on horseback into the furthest black hole, but will assuredly stage his own obliviating Eclipse of his Acolytes become Avatars in their own leper-spotted lights. Syfert will wing off transubstantially into a void of mists, while the Annihilator will undoubtedly never go out with an Eliotian whimper. When the Centre of the small Universe is commandeered, No Name Now will dispose of his despatch, claiming the soon approaching Day as his own. London will fall to the Giant Mob, who in turn will be swallowed up in the arms of a Being far more terrifying even than Beowulf's old adversary – Grendel himself.

The Millennial Countdown was well and truly underway, like a ticking clock before blast-off presaging a cosmic firework display or a Tsunami. Would the Jubilee Line extension to Greenwich be complete before the end of the year? was however a question of the profoundest philosophic importance to all Londoners heaven-bent on securing the best vantage-points from which to witness the greatest extravaganza since the Great Fire! As for the Dome, everyone knew all too well now what the wretched supine flying saucer with a punk haircut contained: a vast mountain-range of air-headed exhibits, ostensibly incorporating the whole of History along with the New Age into the bloated, but self-perpetuating

Blairite Concensus mould! Twenty or so Religions would be commemorated – and not even God knew for quite a while if Christianity was going to be one of them, though if so strictly on a 'level playing-field' as the Euro-Bureaucrats would say, even if the Millennium is a meaningless concept outside of the Christian Calendar and Cosmogeny; not that this should remotely concern Outcasts, who assuredly would not be paying £20 or whatnot for the dubious pleasure – privilege?! – of peering between the garishly sculptured legs of the pea-brained, jet-hued, trendy if trainerless, bionic symbol of so-called multi-ethnic, contemporary British Culture! And as for the Wheel, this was all but forgotten – a last-minute sop to the bread-starved, else stuffed suckers for old Caesar's circuses – Fortune or Misfortune to be spelt and spun on the cyclical tide of Time.

Norman Foster's crypto-Freudian/Fraudian gherkin erection, now commissioned at half the height of its dismissed prototype-predecessor, occupies the phallus-projecting minds of the masses as it climbs in conception alone above the venerated Lady of Threadneedle St. Why fly off to New Zealand to witness the first beginnings of the Trimillennial Dawn, when all these Post-Modern Temples of Artifice are going up in the newly cleansed heart of the greatest City on Earth? – the Epicentre of Evil, ha, ha! This corruption is stale and weak – a gloss on pathos if not the pathos beneath the gloss – in the shrivelled brains of the Nietzschean 'Last Men' of the latest, deformed, Neo-Capitalist Type. True Evil has always proved more magnanimous than this – the garland of Dynasties, no less; Though it must now retreat before its burden of banality to summon the wrath necessary to its highest Historical task.

Bill Gates, for all his famed electronic brain-power, is nonetheless not the Prime Mover of the Planet as he has always affected to believe. He is too near to its Centre of Gravity for this, the Archimedean Principle of leverage from an Outside vantage-point still being as valid now as before, the Lever in question being held obscurely in the hands of mysterious Marginals needing no Mainstream recognition of their self-authorizing potentialities. An earthquake in Turkey was filling up judicious column-inches during the silly season, while dear young – or not so young, as recent stresses and strains have told – Tony and Cherie continued blithely to sun themselves in five square miles of otherwise deserted Tuscan Landscape, there being no politically embarrassing Geological fault-lines there! In Russia, the senile, geriatric bear, Yeltsin – who should have been led into a corner and politely fed long ago – clung all the more desperately to Power the further his second childhood progressed, threatening to crush the Chechnyans once and for all to crown a Millennium of unceasing, if intermittent conflict with the said warrior people. While in America, the Texan Ranger Bush Junior was lining up the unimpeachable Immortal Clinton in his slang-fest sights in readiness for the electoral rigging of a deviant-free zone in his post-Millennial, Bush Family Robinson, Fascist-Republican Dynasty. The East Timorese, for many years condemned to obscurity by virtue of Western, post-Imperial blindness and only relieved of this in perpetuum thanks to Chomsky and Pilger, were now in open revolt against their Indonesian Oppressors – heartened by the News of Suharto's progressive ill-health, though maybe not by his refusal to risk following in the steps of General Pinochet!

And the Dispossessed dreamed on, envisioning the damnation of Democracy.

The net of Nihilism slowly tightened around the jugular of London, squeezing the very last spawn-dregs from the Millennial monster. And the madness of the Populus would be equal to the task of its metamorphosis. The passage of events in the world was perfectly mirrored in London, as Summer subsided into Autumn. An earthquake hit Taiwan. A hurricane hit Florida. Civil War threatened in East Timor. The mouse of Chechnya continued to roar against the Russian Bear. Bio-Terrorism, in the form of toxic mosquitoes, hit New York. Iraq and North Korea forever connived at arsenals of Armageddon. The ghost of General Zia rose again to stamp Martial Law upon the starved Democracy of Pakistan. The sixth billionth baby was born in India. While in London two trains collided. A bus crashed over a bridge. The Real

IRA threatened to detonate the Dome. The Wheel stuck on the diagonal before attaining the vertical during the second lift. The Thames bridges would be no-go areas on the Night. With millions of people thronging the streets on either side of the River, there would be an unstoppable momentum gathering to mount and claim these draw-bridges spanning the moat that split the two halves of London instead of encircling them both. The re-unification of North and South London on the broken Wall of Power would celebrate itself in the burning blood of Royalty, Politicians, Judges, Bureaucrats, Mayors, Councillors and Businessmen, releasing the iron-fisted Mob from the Mandarins' velvet grip.

The bird-carried toxins descended here as everywhere from the sky, to be confounded with angel-dust in the ensuing euphoric mania. The Establishment, Media and Think-Tanks defining current and future agendas and scenarios from the political through the social and cultural to the technological, cannot anaesthetize or deflate the swelling animosity of people possessed at long last of the ENGINE of their own Sovereignty. These budding Leviathans of the Global Underclass can WILL the reversal of Gravity, Newton's black magic powering a subterranean levitation. In all the streets of the City there is at least one Individual or informal cell intent on perpetrating some form of lasting mayhem on the now rapidly approaching Night. And it is not only their own urges and beliefs that bend them hellward, but the morphic suction of force-fields ultimately beyond their control and comprehension. These force-fields are only superficially to do with the Millennium as such or with cosmic fate. Essentially they are to do with the Nihilist-Demiurge's answer to the glut of science and the dearth of culture. If Civilization can no longer deliver – Life too – then it deserves to be destroyed. What will survive is a grotesque inversion of the Christ – a monstrous regeneration that everybody deserves and which only a few can thrive upon.

No Name Now decided to impart one more gift to his Brethren, before taking his sole place in the last star. Their strength vastly enhanced, their immunity to radiation and all other poisons complete, their consumption of entrails and all other matter inedible to their weak human counterparts self-sufficient, they only lacked the ability to inhabit public spaces in perpetuity like astral flesh-demons shifting in and out of the visible realm. Like a cursing shaman-healer passing his hands at supersonic speed over the heads of all those assembled, he graced them with an etherising faculty. Then he spoke his last words to them, reserving a stare of fathomless significance for Syfert in particular. "I am now departing for my Destiny. You will never set eyes on me again, only my signature in scorched landscapes passing through the Eye of the Dark Spirit. But you will survive the coming Meta-Apocalypse with my gift of phantom-mastery. You may use it as you please. Go now and plunder the domains that await you. Resurrect your own mutations from the Dead of Humanity and stride with them across the plains of the Infinite. I have spared you as Outcast-Deities. Toss your boulder-burdens into the Abyss at the base of the summitless Hill. Few others will emulate your hideous supremacy. Spare none that cannot. Human Society has no future. Your Destiny, like my own, is soon to pass in a vast garden of dead stars. This is the Goal of Being, stripped of inessence – the final desire of the boldest, undestroyed atom-rejects of all species, especially the human. I am going to hide in the heart of London, then on the night of my calling I shall plunge the City into the blackness of the collapsing Cosmos."

He did not wait for a reply or a gesture of farewell, but turned swiftly away and vanished through the rear exit – forever beyond their immediate ken. Syfert knew this moment would come and felt gladdened that No Name Now's departure had left them strong and not extinct. In his own domain, he would now truly be King. The Annihilator felt even more relieved, not having suffered the same fate as Dr. Plague. He no longer had to pit himself against a superior foe – the world was now his crater. The remainder felt awe-struck, yet freer than ever before. Obscurius no longer even WANTED to write. There was no work of Art or work of Anti-Art remotely comparable to the total death of life on Earth. That final fact transcended all Scripture, even in the most putrid of media. Creation without destruction was hubris.

To dissolve into Non-Being – to be spread out through its Eternity – was the only foul truth of Art worth living and dying and above all NOT writing for. The writing on the wall spelt the evisceration of body and soul. Those whose bleak core survived this were only arriving at the beginning of Art. Elethea was now the Whore of Babylon writ large, straddling the cockless ball of the Earth – Feminism with a feral face, abominating the foetal plankton of Mankind. Antarctica's white blood would freeze in an instant the steaming plasma from mutilated flesh-mounds. Dr. Plague subsisted in the post-historic fall-out from his inods, his mind's plutonium-life forming nigrescent pools of shadow at the base of some other brain. The War of the Worlds was pending within.

As in a dream of another incarnation, they all departed from their shelter in the wake of No Name Now. But the latter was no longer visible anywhere inside their horizons. Alone of his kind, he had rejoined Himself. And they too were now invisible and impervious to the outside world in the only dimension that mattered – the consummation of their Being. They bade farewell to each other like particles distinct yet never separate, bound to cross each others' paths in the fullness of time. The Titans were now equal to their devastating tasks, each one wedded to a Fate of Civilization. Alone they would remain between the Present and the Post-Millennium, thereafter re-uniting in a global stride with their fellow-survivors of the Ultimate – the magic number of Beings required to optimize their singular License, while still sharing in mutual splendours.

THIRTEEN

Events seem to gather a sinister momentum, in ways that that sleepy, deservedly dead old fathead, Harold Macmillan, could never have imagined. In Armenia, a terrorist coup is staged in Parliament and their leader is shot dead. In America, a plane explodes in the air with over two hundred people on board – a bomb is suspected. In England, a Film-Director portraying Christ as a homosexual – hardly an original theme! – is sentenced to death not by Christian, but Islamic Fundamentalists! A Liberal-Democrat M.P. is also issued with a death-threat for helping to convict the juvenile murderers of another juvenile who would doubtless have murdered his own murderers, had he not been outnumbered! A Yardie crack dealer is shot in Golders Green – of all places! Whatever is the world coming to?! Those for whom either the Brotherhood of Man or the Global Balance of Power are all important considerations, are striving NOT to make significant connections between any such events. Those however with an intransigently Antinomian Agenda – or anti-Agenda – are primed to make of these events what they will. And the awesome malignancy of the movement of Outcasts is spreading faster and further than ever before – from village to town, town to city, city to city, country to country. The dormant anarchy of the Global Underclass is admixed with the active nihilism of Diabolist Illuminati and the toxic angel-dust of mutant contamination. Even Suburbs are crawling with overt, not merely covert weirdness.

The Annihilator knows exactly where he is headed. His hair

shirt arsenal has seeped into and corroded his inhumanly fortified anatomy to such an extent it has become inseparable from it. Like Dr. Plague, his inmortality is assured — but purely as a hideous excrescence from re-combining cyber-organisms. The packed explosives and ammunition beneath his darkened layers of rotted clothing — the fruit of many thefts — have interacted with the radiation to set up a slow time-bomb, which he calculates will explode sui generis not a day or even a second too soon. His intervention in the process of triggering the final, destructive chain-reaction, like the ultra-demonic *deus ex machina*, is no longer even required. He is too monstrous for human recognition. Like an astral Archaeopteryx he storms his flight through London, stealing the quiet of its still conventional citizens, bursting with progeny in every black space it contains. He feeds off his own foul exudations. He has been well-spared by No Name Now. He is now within destroying distance of God. So the man who once took a leaf from Conrad and Dostoyevsky is long forgotten. He has become something OTHER altogether, not needing a human idol of savage perversity, but embodying already the trans-human potentialities of the Meta-Apocalypse. The National Computer is HIS target. He will unleash a Millennium-Bug of his own that will extend to Infinity the two noughts in the year 2000, precipitating the collapse of every other computer and all systems depending on them. Earth's Super-Nova will follow. If he were substantially and continuously visible, he would be seen hovering like the prehistoric bird of prey he has become in and around the region of Wormwood Scrubs. The inmates in the famous or notorious prison nearby have an unsettled sense of his indefinable presence.

Syfert moves with comparable adeptness through the occluded northern hemisphere of London, abandoning the Necronomicon in the astral ashes beneath the flight-path of his phoenix-familiar. When the ladder of Destruction is no longer needed, it can be kicked away. He settles in the alleyways off the Embankment, an elective ghost, within a mile of every centre of power and prestige — from Westminster and Whitehall to the Temple and the Royal Society. He will confound the Scientific Establishment with his magic swallowing of the Light on the Night of momentous glitter. The deathless visitation sleeps and feeds on the paved stomach of the City. The Power-Stations are going to be HIS target. He will jam their supply and transmission through the power in his fingertips. He rears and looms in the shadow-streets like a giant sewage-rat claiming pitiable beggars. The prouder ones he grooms for the Grotesque. The Thames is his ancient reflection, a tidal reservoir of black blood. He swims in it, drinking it down imperceptibly. The thick water seems to admit no light at all. Electricity shies away from its bleak surface. The River of Fire is going to fizzle out in a basin of charcoal soup, dense as cosmic death.

Obscurius spirits himself through unscripted space, staking his territory in the vast industrial wasteground behind Kings Cross. HIS target will be the British Library, the imaginary font of all learning, the inert centre at every universe of discourse. The new building next to St. Pancras housing the British Museum Reading Room has banished the Bloomsbury Mausoleum into Gothic oblivion, cosmetically streamlining all texts in a post-literate, electronic vacuum. He is going to pulp the stored Memory of Mankind into a papier machè of dead signifiers. The threads of Culture will taper off like waxed rope-ends in a Great Abyss. The old Dark Ages spawned a Renaissance of Light from an unbreakable tissue of scholarship. The new Dark Ages will substitute the obscure for the celebrated, reversing the legacies of fame, notoriety and indifference. The strangest Outcasts of all will have pride of place in a reign of grey terror.

Elethea, the Salome of the Supernatural, descends on Soho to eclipse the stale hubris of Sex. This oldest weapon of Woman has been banalized beyond salvation. The primal danger of the act will be released from the greasy hand of Commerce. Mere pleasure is not the goal of Sex, any more than procreation. Sex is a biologically redundant form of suffering. Elethea derives an infinite succour from the decadent glorification of carnal suffering. If Soho is to be her corrupt foundation, celestial Babylon will be her crotch-adorned pedestal. The Whore has razor-tipped wings that fan and scythe the inseminated ether of perversity. This Archetype of irredeemable and shameless filth is now the equal of any Man-Devil, plunging pious Feminists along with idiot Chauvinists into the lowest depths of her vaginal Abyss. She has become the Red Witch of the Earth.

Antarctica heads for the coolest spaces of the City, morgue-freezers and ammonium deposits, spreading her cryogenic frost like Dracula's mist. It is HER contention that an Ice Age will pre-empt Global Warming. The Dinosaurs perished in the last Ice Age. Mankind will perish in the next. Like an encircling asteroid, a gravity chill from deep space, she breathes her bloodless patina over every life-form moving within her ken. The iceberg that destroyed the Titanic on its maiden-voyage has shifted through many configurations and dimensions to become Her in its coldest essence. A thousand Titanics of Civilization will break up against her razor-crystal form, as she rises like a silver Atlantis from the oceans of the Night. The heat-sources of the City slowly deplete as she plots her passage from the suburbs to the inner city. Westminster feels as cold as High Barnet on a winter's day. The exponential accumulation of her powers has resulted from the ominous grace of No Name Now's intervention.

As for No Name Now, he has gone ahead of them all, returning to his earthly roots in East London. If he was inapprehensible in the past, he belongs to another order or index of inapprehensibility now. His long dead maternal abductress is utterly absorbed into the scattered effluent of his indestructible physiognomy, her 'case' long closed and abandoned. He flits between invisible astral essences and hideous, half-human forms with the effortless ease of an Absolute Deity. The Isle of Dogs, or that part of it which still remains a wilderness, draws him to it like a microcosmic dot on the vast magnet that attaches him to his origins. The Millennium Dome across the water is well within pulverizing distance. If for a long time there was nothing in it, then quite soon there will be nothing left of it! There is no excuse for waiting twenty five years to dismantle it! And what the Real IRA will be unable to destroy with explosives, No Name Now will reduce to fibrillated rubble with a mere flicker of his terrible hand. He ranges through every manifestation known to Demonology across the estuarial hinterlands, biding his prophetic time in the least known wastelots of the world. HIS rest is that of the Great Destroyer.

FOURTEEN

What has always crudely been called the 'countdown phase' is now entered upon. A haze of anticipation, both joyful and fearful, descends overs Civilization during this period. The surface events of Politics or Current Affairs seem to drift into abeyance, as if their topical importance such as it ever is were overshadowed by a momentous and Historic fixation. A symptom of the burgeoning mayhem is the increased incidence of mass-shootings in different countries, often by teenagers. In Jerusalem, security-forces are rounding up Messianists who take the prospect of the Second Coming just a little too literally for the Authorities' liking. Everybody in Power affects the duplicitous air of appearing to want everybody else to have both a stupendously ecstatic and a transcendently meaningful EXPERIENCE on the night. But in truth, they are shivering in their poshly disguised jack-boots at the prospect of what may befall them.

Advance-Intelligence has of course been gathered by the Police and Security concerning the broad cross-spectrum of anarchic disturbances and worse that are being planned to coincide with the otherwise innocuous Jubilation ahead. The military will be at the ready in the event of a mass riot in London, as elsewhere. A mortality-rate of approximately one thousand is predicted and so a special mortuary has been prepared on a sporting-ground near the Dome. This forecast reveals so little of true intelligence as to be quietly risible. Even the Mohawks of organizations like Class War, with their primitive boxes of tricks and alternative combat-camouflages, will claim many more lives than this. And as for the Elect of the Outcasts – untraced and not even suspected by the most talent fed and tenacious of the 'watchers' from the Ruling Establishment's most secret Agencies – mere Statistics will cower and collapse before the sheer magnitude of their imminent atrocities. The Wheel will spin astronomically out of control, sending each of the thirty two gondolas carrying twenty five passengers sailing on a far from idyllic Venetian ride through the rather more Venusian rings of flame belching through the Earth's atmosphere into the farthest recesses of outer space. The entire voting-membership of the House of Commons and the House of Lords could be granted free one-way tickets for their last ride together into the Great Unknown, given the enormous seating capacity on this circus-megalith. What a truly satisfying, final tribute to Popular Democracy they'd be paying, by making this noblest of all sacrificial gestures!

The Peasants' Revolt and Cade's Rebellion, the Gordon Riots and the Poll Tax Riots are all examples of uprisings – involving the unruliest elements in the English Class-system – that occurred in London. They are the Historical precursors of the Millennial Mayhem to come. But the latter is going to reveal a supernatural dimension unprecedented in the other insurgencies. And it is this dimension that will guarantee its success, rather than Ideology or Technology. Only its success will not be followed by the unfolding of any Utopian blueprint. Instead, an Olympian Egoism is going to reign supreme in a blasted environment without any social fabric. The most deranged and deformed Individuals will come into their own element and the masses will succumb or perish. History will be superseded. Tony Blair still struts his stuff like some tenth-rate Media creation of a Macchiavellian Prince masquerading as a caring Christian and a man for all seasons, a centre-stage clown facing every way at once. The true megalomaniac is revealed behind the cosmetic facade of the charismatic Reformer. His bubble is on the verge of bursting, like the swollen head he possesses – soon to splatter his spin-doctored brains all over his wretched Cabinet-cronies in an unwitting, not to say useless imitation of Dr. Plague. And beneath the caricaturing rictus of the religiously rehearsed toothpaste smile, he is terrified – not at the prospect of that prematurely aged, baseball-capped Yorkshireman at his gate winning the next election, but rather at the very different prospect of that newt-fancying, red-spotted, past master of entryism usurping the post of Mayor and then sticking a monumental spoke in New Labour's merry wheel of fortune. That grey-bearded old pit-bull of the Centre Left is despatched to deal the loony-Bolshie heretic-traitor a deadly bite. While between them that prancing saviour of great white elephants, whose only excuse for being Mayor is honouring his promise never to write any more abysmal books, dances and grins like an imaginary puppet-master. With this trio of tin-pot triumphalists contesting the most powerful future post in London, some violently surreal counter-blast is DEMANDED of its disaffected population almost as a matter of logical necessity.

The disillusionment with Politics and Life in general is mounting to the same pitch achieved in the sixties and seventies, only with the added potency of the Millennial fission building to its critical level. No self-confessed Rationalist believes a miracle is going to transform the world on the Night. The Day of Judgement could theoretically fall on any Day – or else no Day as such but the summation of all Days or the Day of Days, a Day outside of Time or a Day of special Eternity. Or there will not be a Day of Judgement – or Atonement, or Deliverance. There is just some more or less infinite Continuum, and that is all. So why divide Time up into Millennia? Only a political Religion would have any purpose or Agenda behind such an act of Chronological despotism. It helps to create the illusion of a clear understanding of History, and it keeps Mankind in a state of subjection to the tyranny of Authority – the fear of what is foretold. What better occasion to sweep all this spiritually and intellectually crippling crap away, than just such an occasion itself?

The Nietzschean power of the will is the most potent force in the Universe, superseding Science and History in its passionate manipulation of nature. Those Humans emancipated from morality and transfigured into Beings greater than mortal animals or soulful angels can become as licentious demon-gods creating their own Laws in a sublime disharmony. The Man-God and the God-Man are cancelled in an awesomely bestial unnameability. The miracle that is going to happen is the miracle that can and will be MADE by the multitude of risen Outcasts tearing the burden of a crushing Civilization from their shoulders and hurling it into the deepest Abyss. And this will indeed APPEAR to be a miracle of Gargantuan proportions to the uninitiated, even though it will leave behind none of the stigmata of reverential ritual – the blessed marks of imponderable divinity. It won't be a miracle in a Christian, or in any religious sense of this much-abused word. It will be an active unfolding of magnificent maleficence.

The Luddite farm-labourers in nineteenth century England smashed the products of the Machine Age. The Industrial Revolution truly broke the age-old Agrarian mould. But Technology is less the enemy than Technocracy of course. Tools are our servants, not our masters. And if the Luddites had no articulate response to the tools that were supplanting their stock-in-trade, their sense of grievance at being sacrificed on the altar of sudden Progress after centuries of comparative cyclical stability was perfectly understandable. Today however we are inured to the effects of exponential advancement. It is the invasion and conquest of our inner selves by Technology, as well as our outer behaviour and ways of life, that brings forth the neo-Luddite-Rebel in us. As such, it is never stupid to oppose an alien System which seeks to re-define our identities for us on its own supremely arbitrary terms of reference. The act of smashing computers will be an act of reclamation, since what have computers done for the majority of people they were designed to serve? NOTHING. They profit the Elite who understand their workings, and few if any others.

Smashing buildings, or certain buildings, will also be an act of reclamation for all those oppressed and manouevred against their wills by Modern Architects and the Powers-that-be who colonize the buildings housing the Institutions they preside over. Not only is the Land or Space reclaimed, but also the very symbolism of Power and Authority which can be reconverted thereby into tangible freedom – the Sovereignty of the Subject with a capital S. The Forms of Society that evolve on this foundation may not even stem from cooperation at all. If Individuals can be Societies unto themselves, then this may be all that they ever wish for. The people can go to Hell, or Heaven, or neither – in their own way, of course. The largely forgotten French Situationists behind Les Evenements in Paris, in May 1966, developed such ideas as these in a post-Marxist climate of opinion. Although not acknowledged, their influence is resurging in subtly unexpected ways after three decades of an atavistic slump in which the tautly strung threads of their far-reaching Dialectic could not be sustained and a period of dull Reaction with only superficial variations set in. Those people hell-bent on massively disrupting the organized party on the Night – whether graced with the toxin-curse of No Name Now and his independent Brethren or not – are the witting or unwitting beneficiaries of both Luddism and Situationism. And they will vindicate the relative failures of these great undercurrents in a feast of SUCCESS that will owe nothing in essence to either Capitalism or Communism.

And even the act of killing people – certain people – will be one of reclamation too. The true Peace of an emancipated Populus, rather than the spurious, conflict-ridden Peace of that German, stamp-adorning figure-head, can and will ensue from the ultimate revisitation of violence upon those who visited the original acts of violence on everybody else – upon those whose violence lies buried and superficially unrecognized in centuries of legitimated crime stretching far behind them, beneath ill-begotten estates propping up seats of privilege. Of what use is and in what virtue resides morality, when it serves merely as an apologetic for the vast, hidden offenses of the Ruling against the Ruled? Does the notion of killing such people seem so terribly WRONG, when one considers how totally their crimes eclipse the crimes of those they routinely arraign and punish? If a Judge can condemn a man, cannot the man condemn the Judge? Why is the act of killing such a moral stumbling-block in the Human Mind, when it has been so liberally indulged in throughout Human History? The abstruse and the sentimental can ponder these issues forever. But the History makers have resolved them by decisive action. So also will the History UNMAKERS – the Post-Historic Anarchs – on the Night.

London suffers under the systematic onslaught of Millennial construction and councillor-palm-greasing, autotrophic Property Development. The completed Jubilee Line extension will convey the ultra-sensation seekers in glittering cattle-trucks to the fun-palace/concentration-camp at Greenwich. The Covent Garden Opera House must be open in time, the stretched slab of an adjoining Complex on the ancient site of Lundenwich demonstrating finally that Architectural and Aesthetic Imagination DIED ten years before. An extra-terrrestrial block of flats has arisen like a spaceship from the Thamesis – or Thorney Island – upriver from Westminster on the North Bank. Private flats are going up all over the City like a rash of vain indulgences. It's like the Eighties all over again. There's nothing like a new Millennium it seems, to galvanize people out of the longest recession in living memory. New Labour may have abandoned the THEORY of boom and bust cycles, pace Gordon Brown's dour mantra, but dispassionate observers KNOW that such cycles cannot simply be eradicated with a little budgetary tinkering and the invocation of some macro-economic theoretical gobbledegook. Real poverty not only still exists, but is starkly visible in the faces and clothes of London's and Britain's growing – grown – army of post-neo-capitalist, socio-economic casualties. The lie of collective emancipation reflects blindingly off the savage hollows of their eyes.

The property-boom is a sure Lottery for the minority of City-clowns, Web nerds and Networking wankers, while the majority sink slowly – or not so slowly – into the clay silt at the slump-end of the market. The Logic of the present trend leads to the conclusion that in the next century a cupboard, or even a shoe-box, will cost a quarter of a million pounds – always assuming there is a property market left. In which case, the way is paved for a great Rachmanite resurgence. And as for the average person's pension, it will scarcely even buy a meal in twenty years time – courtesy of

New Labour's predictable failure to control inflation. And no other political party will fare any better. Politics is increasingly impotent to affect, still less change, anything of a fundamental nature. Only something truly catastrophic can radically alter the unconscionably cynical and utterly crass course on which the latest deformed model-machine of Global Capitalism is so ineluctably set. After Reform, Revolution used to be considered by some as the only ultimate remedy for the casual iniquities of a system totally out of control, governed only by its own insane and unstoppable momentum. But Revolution today is at worst a Totalitarian stain on History and at best a forgotten joke.

However, Revolution will yet prove to be the initial condition of a transformation unconceived and unimagined by the intellectual and moral guardians and arbiters of all Utopian blueprints – the past Popes of failed or semi-failed secular religions. Marx and Nietzsche have always been mentioned in the same breath by the more bestial Romantics of Revolutionary Philosophy and Praxis, even though the former unwittingly bequeathed the legacy of the Gulag and the latter the legacy of Auschwitz. Marx, both visionary and analyst, struggled in the dark to move towards the light. Is he to be condemned in perpetuity for articulating the worldview that would be twisted out of all recognition by some of those who followed in his wake, like megalomanic dwarves standing on the shoulders of a powerless giant? One may as well condemn Christ for the Inquisition. And as for Nietzsche, he would have squirmed in his coffin at the sight of a bunch of bone-headed goose-steppers raiding his works like rats in a larder for epigrams they could convert into the crudest of slogans. The Superman was worlds apart from the blond beast. He was Nietzsche's crowning tribute to Plato's Philosopher-King, while the blond beast was a mere sublimation ot the Archetypal, brainless Thug. The language of heady idealism is no longer spoken or written by anybody with power or influence. Those few who still seek to guard it against consignment have been pushed to the margins of debate and deliberation. And yet the wilderness, being the most intellectually respectable place of all, has sprouted the weed-forests of a fantastical retaliation against the stagnant economic pragmatism of political parties devoid of Philosophy.

The stale contentment and stratified inertia of conservatism with a small 'c' only satisfies suburban minds and frigid bureaucrats. Those possessed of imagination and intellect, spirit and passion combined will risk instability for adventure, Dystopia for Utopia. The Zeitgeist and the Status-Quo are supremely dispensable bog-trends. The corrupt and incompetent chaos of the prevailing conditions is crying out in desperation for an injection of the fresh and inspired chaos of a higher movement of ideas and actions. In this process, Reason must be dipped, if not drowned in the blood of Unreason. The Revolution of everyday Life is ultimately the only true work of Art. And if London remains the epicentre of Life, pace Johnson, the surreal transfiguration of its landscape in the Post-Millennial moment and phase will explode its ripples across the Earth and without cease into the Cosmos beyond – its echoes forever returning, like the pulsar waves of background radiation. What if anything will remain of London on January the first, 2000? This is not a matter for phoney prophets and parlour-game players. It is in the hands of happening.

FIFTEEN

After his long, deceptive march from Whitechapel, No Name Now had slipped invisibly through the Westminster Bridge barrier that had been erected by Government fiat, to take up his self-allocated position at the centre of a now far from Wordsworthian universe. His presence is not even felt or sensed by anyone, official or unofficial; for this is all to the purpose. He has not long to wait however, since crowds as visible to him as he is not visible to them begin to gather like the survivors of some huge calamity clinging together for comfort at the End of History. A strange silence envelops them as though they were about to witness God's funeral procession, their nervous coughs punctuating a laughless solemnity. In truth, an almost unprecedentedly extravagant show is shortly being laid on for this multitude. But it seems beforehand not to have human stage-managers, as if shadowy figures moving permanently behind the breath-taking screens were magicking a mirage into being. They even wonder, vaguely or not so vaguely, at their own humanity and what might potentially become of them in a few hours time. The enormity of History seems to weigh on them with all its pain and dilemmas, as well as its joys and achievements and somewhat desperate hopes for the future. This scene resembles an elevation of Lourdes into the Celestial City.

Sufferers of every disease known to Man permit themselves to half-expect a cure. Mystics of every variety WHOLLY expect to see angelic forms appear in the night-sky above them which are NOT the by-products of collective hallucinations. Satanists of the black-as-sin variety equally expect to behold a power-cut. The widest mix of mankind crushes slowly into the restricted street-spaces subject to the largest police-cordon operation ever mounted in the Capital's history. Whether the fixed boundaries can accommodate with their inflexible entrance and exit points the expected three million viewers of the Night's Spectacle remains to be seen. Families, groups of friends and colleagues, Syndicates, loners losing or finding themselves in the crowd, petty criminals, patient or not so patient revellers, looters, vandals, rioters, street-fighters, muggers, killers and worse – far, far worse – assemble in the largest open Arena ever filled or to be filled in the annals of recorded time.

Only about half the population of London is staying indoors tonight. Some doubtless genuinely prefer the privacy of a small gathering, or perhaps even solitude, on occasions such as this. They can watch the proceedings on Television, Cable or Satellite, feeling vicariously almost as much pleasure or else plain curiosity as do the participants they observe from a position of armchair safety. A surging crowd is not an enjoyable experience, as anybody who has attended the Notting Hill Carnival or the Trafalgar Square New Year celebrations knows – and THIS crowd is something else altogether. Some cynics will probably be taking tranquilizers powerful enough to knock them out for three or four days. They have the right idea, these terminal resistors of the duping allure of saccharine displays and epochal exhibitions. But they are not likely to remain undisturbed, even under these anaesthetizing effects, by the truly astounding events that are soon going to unfold. In fact, nobody anywhere is likely to escape the tidal-flames of Insurrection breaking out in all directions from the fathomless deeps of the greatest profane conurbation ever to evolve on Earth. London is the dark heart of a doomed Cosmos.

The weather is burgeoningly dramatic – dry but disfigured with mountainous clouds, the last fallen sun of the old Millennium giving way to obscurely menacing hints of moon and stars. A dark backcloth to the ubiquitous, brilliantine illuminations holds in store the fullest import and purport of a post-Wagnerian, sturm-und-drang, tragic-romantic Gotterdammerung. The brooding dusk filtered all about can never be eliminated by the high-searching glare and gleam of the vast, electric City. If Aliens are waiting to respond in kind, or otherwise, to the signals intentionally or unintentionally transmitted into the Great Nothingness beyond the Planet, then they are wholly content to stay lurking in or behind the rolling fortifications of condensed acid above men's heads. They may yet confuse the issue of the Second Coming – or the Third Coming, strictly speaking – even more than Christ himself. And as for the Anti-Christ, heralding the ultimate synthesis of the Meta-Christ, he continues incubating his worst ever Incarnation in the remotest space of inner withdrawal as the sounds of excited apprehension begin to multiply and swell among the Crowd. Night thickens and blackens for the last time in History – to endure forever thereafter. The Thames is alive with preparation for the corgi-loving Leviathan and her gaffe-prone Consort, for when they later proceed downriver towards Tower Bridge in the last hour of Time. Whether or not Big Ben completes its twelve chimes on the hour BEFORE the River of Fire is commenced by the Queen's hand – as has been disputed with Broadcasters – is a matter of the sublimest inconsequence in all realms ungoverned by the protocols of Grand Ceremony.

Broadcasting is triumphant in the last allotted hours of its pompous and far from circumstantial reign. It had better make the very most and best of its unwitting swan-song. For Truth is now in the ascendant, as Deception wavers with vertigo. Satellites have linked up all over the Globe like glad hands shaking on the ultimate, phoney Deal. Celebrity performers of all varieties, not least Variety, are inwardly preparing themselves before taking their final few calming breaths on the threshold of stepping out into the Global limelight for that pre-hyped performance of a lifetime. At the other end of the spectrum, the Archbishop of Canterbury – that bottle-brained patron-saint of earnest Evangelism – secretly chokes on the enormity of the occasion, feeling quite powerless to summon its significance in a few agonizingly chosen words of address. The Pope by contrast, will need only to mumble, gesticulate and yawn in his far more pregnant appeal to a universal following from the pop-star-podium of God's vicar resting on a long-dead fisherman's Apocryphal Foundation. The Prime Minister is rehearsing to perfection a Rory Bremner impersonation of a prime minister impersonating the Prophet Moses making up his Ten-Point Programme on Mount Pleasant, Mount Sinai being too Old Labour a platform from which to deliver the speech that will launch or augment his thousand year reign. David Dimbleby is trying to picture himself as his father reporting the Festival of Britain, while dear ole Trevor Macdonald plans to recover his outbred roots as England's favourite well-spoken Uncle Tom.

Bob Geldof's Fireworks are in place, ready at the lighting of touchpaper to burn the currency of England in the highest and widest conflagration of colour ever to burst across the local night-sky – in far higher quantities than on the occasion of the first performance of Handel's music for RoyalFire works in the eighteenth century. What better way to waste public money than to throw it in the air? Many of the Dignitaries and VIPs not called upon to make a public appearance, speech or gesture have carefully pre-selected and pre-arranged their company, activities and Venues for the Night, well away from scrutiny, disturbance and danger. Others however are already mingling as anonymously as they can contrive in the great ant-colony of the Crowd, its collective brain focused on higher or lower things than the mere recognition of well-known public faces. These figures will be among the first then to have visited upon them the suddenly released store of wrath simmering just below the surface in the psyche of the Populus, awaiting only the explosive trigger of the Midnight Toll to ignite the fuse of Momentous Destiny.

No Name Now prepares to assume visible form – the most terrible apparition ever to show its face to Mankind, arising in the direct path-line of the vertical column of sparks racing up the River to complete its course in the estimated ten seconds. His Brethren have positioned themselves at strategic points on a pentacle of power superimposed as a symbolic map of malign magic on the City. In all the closed Institutions – the prisons, hospitals and asylums – the inmates and patients are ravenous for liberty, sensing the hand of deliverance fanning the winds that are blowing outside their locked and barred windows. Even those confined in their own homes are inciting primal fears of cataclysmic storms, collapsing systems and structures razed to the ground. Every man paints his own picture of Armageddon in the incommunicable privacy of his innermost vision. Alcohol is playing its generous part in slowly drowning out such gnawing terrors, disinhibiting the restrained majority and plunging them into a flood of excessive urges. These urges will play into the hands of the many extremist factions in the crowd's midst, armed for the greatest battle of all and growing louder in their chants by the minute.

If Time can be wrenched out of its course by the sheer intensity of motion building up, then there can be little doubt that this is going to happen on the far side of Midnight – if not on the near side. Even the postulates of High Energy Physics stipulate and support this hypothesis. All over the City the churches are filling up, the mood of sombre mystery among the extraordinary congregations subsiding into one of evangelical exhilaration. The bells start ringing out like an Epiphany of Byzantine echoes. The Moment is nearing – that indefinable, infinitely divisible yet fundamentally indivisible, discreetly inexperiencable yet fleetingly experienced, eternal yet barely existent INSTANT – and those not too drunk or drugged or otherwise intoxicated to even notice it as such, will assuredly be struck dumb in rather more than the mere Biblical sense before welling out their very deepest quintessence of joy, awe, frustration, remorse, anger, hatred and devastation. Every emotion known to Man, and a few not yet known, will become acutely manifest.

Syfert has already staked his territory on the far side of Tower Bridge, swimming ectoplasmically downriver from the Embankment to claim the backcloth to London's Great Sham-Show for the risen, black-fleshed Chthulhu of his own singular conjuring. The Annihilator is simultaneously liberating the incarcerated scum of Wormwood Scrubs as a prelude to a domino-effect rippling through all the other prisons, inciting a mass-riot after passing through the outer wall to emanate within in the tall guise of Satan.

He eviscerates and gobbles up the Governor and guards in a manner worthy of Grendel, or Dracula coming for Renfield, and then finally explodes the famous twin-pillared Entrance with a powdered curse all his own. The rabble is thus released to claim the City for itself, while the Annihilator slips through Space to decimate the very nerve-centre of the Nation-State. Obscurius has spread his grey wings across the dying flats of St. Pancras and Somers Town, secreting himself into the British Library and consuming the entire corpus of literature or waste-product of good trees in the voluminous folds of his spectral stomach. He then squats semi-visibly on top of the roof of the Building, a fitting ironic adornment to the slag-pile of modern architecture, emitting the bio-degraded gases of the great scriptural canon far and wide – right to the very horizons of his poisoned sights His vocation has reached its apogee.

Dr. Plague meanwhile has reassembled himself in the sewers as a species of strung out, irradiated plesiosaur, accelerating the breakdown of Joseph Bazalgette's long-suffering gut-child as he expands toward the Hemisphere of the Above-Ground. Elethea and Antarctica have struck a Dialectical balance of local and universal temperatures, the former's steam of lust tensely counterpointing the latter's mist of unfeeling like matter and anti-matter not quite colliding, but coming perilously near at the alpha and omega point of creation and destruction, the continuum and origin. Soho bursts into flame as the Thames freezes over for something other than a Dutch-inspired cloth-fair or a skating promenade. The mounting rumble of these crisis-ruptures at outlying regions of the West End and City gradually reaches the ears of the millions now gathered near the River. The ground begins to shake beneath their feet, as if a fleet of tumbrils is converging upon them, opening cracks in the earth. Violent mayhem is already erupting just BEFORE the Moment has arrived – not after – in the threatened terms of strict Chronological Time. The anticipation of the Moment has actually created a fearsome glitch – an alternative Time, a parallel-universe the far side of a worm-hole in space, an imaginary reality supplanting all Cosmological measurement.

The Royal Cargo voyaging up the River is beset with obstacles in the form of ice-traps laid for them by the breathless, working magic of Antarctica. They cannot be airlifted at such short notice, even though Police helicopters are at the ready. So it has become a race against Time to reach Tower Bridge in Time, where Syfert is lying in wait for them. No Name Now however wants the Sovereign specimens to complete their journey, because it is essential to his ultimate coup that the River of Fire commences as and when planned and then travels as far as him. So he subverts Antarctica's conspiracy of ice with a sudden, imperceptible flash of heat warming up the River and melting the ice with an unnatural speed – to the stunned amazement of the Royal Couple and their escorts. They can only explain it to themselves as a freak-effect of the amassed body-temperatures of the nearby crowds or else some miraculous portent of the occasion. They feel themselves borne on a magic carpet in an open-air Styx.

As the boat nears its destination, the noise of the crowd reaching a Heaven-splitting pitch and Big Ben recording the last minutes of the eleventh hour, No Name Now manifests in a compression of cosmic effluence, a supremely frightful mutilation of gravity. The City galvanizes in a hallucinatory frisson of churning dimensions. Just as the police and military are preparing to tackle the puzzling outbreaks of anarchy on the outskirts of the West End before they can move in towards the centre, everybody flips onto a wavelength of uncontrollable insanity – EXCEPT the Royal Couple and their entourage, who like figures in a pageant move in suspended animation through their procedural paces. Big Ben is not yet stopped, even though Greenwich Meantime has ceased to signify. The mighty clock has become a Talisman of Terror. All the tyrants great and small, and their ranks of minions and lackeys, remain just sane enough to be appallingly AFRAID of the otherwise fearless insanity that surrounds them and which is now coming for them in the shape of a Diabolical army of supra-fortified malcontents. An eerily awesome period of calm precedes the Cosmic storm about to break with the first shattering chime of the clock that received its first broadcast exactly seventy seven years ago. No Name Now commands everything, the moods of the Populus and the ordering of events. So it is HE who now synchronizes the movement of the Queen's hand as she prepares to release the dazzling, fizzling sheet of flame that has mesmerized people's anticipations for so long with the mechanical shifting of component-parts producing the Byzantine boom of the thirteen ton bell, the great pride and joy of the old Whitechapel Foundry near to the scene of his recent haunts. What follows condemns description.

Like an ominous Angel of Mons, he spreads across the Night – ready to stop and absorb the tidal shark-fin of laser-light now racing towards him, accompanied by the life-stilling rhythm of the twelve strikes and the momentarily delayed quasar-crescendo of the Crowd. In an oscillating phase or vortex-rupture, he appears to fry and blaze with white radiance, trailing a dead space behind him. The spark-sprites that fly off him in all directions enter the bodies and souls of the people for miles around, as they ignite the buildings of London in a panoramic Hologram of Hell. Rationality and Rule, as they are constituted in reified form, are suspended along with Time and orchestrated occurrence. Space convulses and the maddened minotaurs of the mob take possession of London. God only knows what the Establishment and the Media are now thinking and doing. None of this matters any more, as the only issue of importance is what the Promethean Magi of the Moment are creating – and perhaps more to the immediate point, DESTROYING. The sub-Epicurean hedonists, the materialistic partying paparazzi, find themselves swiftly and overwhelmingly eclipsed by the violently deranged and magically powered paupers, misfits and rebels of the eternal contemporary. A savage roar travels through the City like a column of rain. Lights go out everywhere as supplies fail and break down. Only fire and the unearthly cynosure of No Name Now's revealed presence illuminate the suffocating nigredo of the Night.

It is quite clear to those who can still think that rather more than the Millennium-Bug is responsible for what is happening. An horrendous inversion of the Second Coming has ACTUALLY visited the Earth against all the logical odds, they conclude in isolated unison. The National Computer fries into extinction, reducing to a black cinder-chip of all its accumulated data of rigidly stratified, Hierarchical oppression, obliterated at one glorious stroke beneath the exploding impact of the Annihilator's Animus. A state of emergency is cobbled together and urgently communicated with any available means, including sirens, by the battered and reeling powers-that-be. Convoys are mobilized amidst a rapid chaos of messages and instructions, criss-crossing like acac-fire over the Mandarins' no-man's-land. It is unclear who is safe and who is not – even the Royal Couple have mysteriously vanished, whether in a helicopter or the maw of No Name Now's avenging mission no one can publicly say or privately knows. The scene is being replicated in every major conurbation on the planet, the toxic birds having delivered their gifts, extending the force fields from the nucleus-core of the Outcast-Elects. The physical structures of so-called civilized life are suffering a catastrophe analogous to a continental shift or the War of the Worlds without corny aliens.

In the streets of London, two main tendencies are manifesting. Individuals are going completely berserk in their own separate spaces, shrieking and shaking and tearing at their clothes, clawing the air around them as if it were filled with visible, tangible demons. At the same time, groups are forming according to no prescribed patterns, marauding and charging, pillaging and ravaging every obstacle in sight, be it human, animal or inert. They have grown superhumanly strong, feeling themselves impregnable against all opposition. In the Strand for instance, the oldest street in London and scene of every aspect of human life in the past, from rough trading and trafficking through fashionable decorum and dandified, decadent display to riotous bestiality, the sound of shattered glass carries acoustically on the air like an avalanche, a shower of detonated icicles. Not a single Shop, Office, Hotel, Bank, Theatre, Restaurant, Cafe or Cinema is spared the frenzied rape of property that is gathering pace and pouring out of the Populus like boiling bile. Anyone caught up in the surging, seething mass of reclamatory beasts, who is only there for the occasion, the spectacle of a good time – or worse still as a mere bystander or trapped passer-by – is either transfigured by the experience or destroyed by it, trampled and crushed underfoot, pulped and slashed where they stand. The police and the military cannot as yet penetrate this giant herd of driven bodies. Such is the force and intensity of their demonic possession that it is to be doubted whether tear-gas or even bullets can stop them in their tracks. Nothing short of the most extreme measures will have the remotest chance of checking them. The ghosts of the burnt or mutilated victims of the Peasants' Revolt, clinging to this haunted ground between the medieval Charyng Village and the Savoy Palace, re-awaken beneath the affray to surface and mingle with the dislodged spirits of the living. While up above them a nocturnal vision infinitely worse than the Apocalypse and the Last Judgement combined takes inexorable and abominable shape.

There seems little point in looting, for it is dawning on the participants that there will be no Economy in which to re-circulate the goods stolen during the aftermath of this terminal uprising. Nothing that cannot be cannibalized or pressed into the service of extermination is worth stealing. Everything in the alienating Hierarchy, and everybody holding it up, is only there to be pulverized into a nullity. The most unrestrained primal instincts of ancient man are wedded to the infernal powers of Beings transcending the limits of nature and humanity. If the Blitz had reduced parts of London to moon-like craters, the Millennium-Riots as they may henceforth be known in some hypothetical future, will reduce the WHOLE of London to the state of a dead star – short of a saving grace from some member of the Outcast-Elect. And the sight of buildings being literally torn down with bare hands, smashed in with any available weapon and kicked through with fortress-shattering ferocity, already confirms the unfolding truth of this scenario. The Savoy Hotel suffers this fate, being far from 'the fairest mansion in all England' like its palatial predecessor on the same site over six hundred years before. The besieged tycoons are unceremoniously dismembered, their body-parts then burned to unrecognition along with the building itself.

However the Savoy Chapel is spared, due to Syfert's sudden intervention, the pauper Inigo Jones's little gem re-possessed as a cathedral for the dispossessed in the surreal landscape to come.

Syfert disposes of modern architecture, the South Bank Complex being an imperative no longer to be delayed, while the Millennium Dome can await his attentions as a fitting finale to the dissolution of all philistine structures. The Annihilator destroys all Government buildings, Bureaucratic headquarters – and unaesthetic churches. And No Name Now dispenses with the rest. What WILL be left of London is the most beautiful skeletal extraction of its obscurest essence. Obscurius ensures the preservation of St. Pancras Station from a misdirected assault by the Kings Cross street-mob – though not out of admiration for Scott, whose neo-Gothic masterpiece resulted from a fluke of misplaced inspiration. St. Pancras SHOULD have been designed by Waterhouse. The Foreign Office is belching up treacly flames furlongs high, spreading a mushroom of smoke over Whitehall in which the spiritual observer can detect the ashen resurrection of Henry the Eighth's Colossus amongst palaces. A sheet of fire rushes above head-height down Whitehall, from the Treasury to the Admiralty, Richmond Terrace to the Ministry of Agriculture – a pearl-necklace of nihilism. The transported marauders below are desensitized to the heat, releasing so much heat of their own as to cool their flesh almost to the point of inuring themselves against burns. The heavily policed barrier across Downing St. is crashed through like a ring of fire, and the Seat of the Prime Prick of England and his Secret Cabinet is swarmed over and swept through like a leftover Augean Stable summoning a new Race of Herculeans in a post-Herculean Age. Since 1734, this home and office of ignominious autocracy and oligarchy has held sway over a far too acquiescent Populus – but not any more. The ashes of Authority pile up on the grave of Government. The Cabinet Office nearby, the HQ of the Privy Councillors, is successfully stormed this time, after the anarchist coup foiled in the last century. The organs of State are crushed, one by one.

The Houses of Parliament are of course no strangers to fire

or bombs, albeit of the Fascist rather than the Anarchist variety. The fourth fire in their turbulent history will however be the last. No phoenix of arbitrary or elective Power will rise from the ashes of this barbarous monolith. A sight that would have brought tears of joy to Guy Fawkes's eyes – though no Papist conspirator has a hand in THIS conflagration – now fills the space that once framed the great neo-Gothic conceit, with flakes swirling strangely around Big Ben, which still stands in a black air repelling the darting dragon-tongues of Destiny. Westminster Abbey meets its own incendiary fate, no longer fore-closed by fortune's rescue. Fire and darkness have long been the weapons of revolt, but water is now added as the fuming acidic clouds suddenly break to release an unnatural fall of rain. Normally, such a body of water would swamp the momentum of a riot. But this time it creates a mood of frenzied rebirth – a mutant baptism. And the fires are not dampened so much as aggravated like seething fat, the steaming plasma of human flesh buoyed up in the atmosphere by the explosive force of the flames fanned by the unholy winds.

Pitched battles of superhuman ferocity break out all over the City, the police and armed forces increasingly estranged from their command and their sense of official Identity even, as they get gradually sucked into a maelstrom of indiscriminate destruction. They are fighting for their lives and even against each other as much as against an identifiable enemy or target. The cosmically crazed pandemonium engenders a war of each against each. Heads roll in the streets while bodies are mangled to a pulp. Vehicles are burnt out or pulverized. Telekinetic demons race across the skies, spinning objects out of orbit, wrenching matter from its sockets. The Annihilator swoops like an astral ghoul to claim a policeman here, a soldier there, cadre-cadavers everywhere. Syfert swells the River into a tidal wave of foaming blood and the murky silt of drowned legions, crashing like Krakatoa's displacement over the banks and boroughs of a fallen City. Obscurius has asphyxiated whole swathes of the population of North London with his crowning response to Life and Literature, sinking centripetally into the subterranean slime of the last neo-Babylonian

Empire, an omniverous Quatermass monster engorging the conceits of culture in a final speechless gesture. Elethea and Antarctica have cancelled each other out like matter and anti-matter meeting unavoidably, restoring a reign of nothingness that will refill gradually with an order of existence barely precedented in the one that went before it.

No Name Now has spread himself out through the inner integuments of Space, the black magician of a blinding Void. The contours of the City are irrevocably altered, the whole landscape resembling Hiroshima with stranded towers. The entire architectural superstructure of Business and Bureaucracy has been pounded into the clay crust of a lost Civilization. A fate worse than nuclear or bio-chemical obliteration has befallen the great Citadel of the Globe. The buildings and people have suffered slowly and a terrible new life emerges from the devastation. Swift oblivion would have been far kinder, but then the Avengers of the Damned would never have had the perverse satisfaction of their amoral retribution. London is now a mirror of the world, as the survivors of the Meta-Apocalypse wander like dazed giants across a war-torn terrain not seen on Planet Earth since the extinction of the Dinosaurs sixty million years earlier.

Appalling tortures are visited on the remaining pockets of official resistance, their entrails ripped out of them and drunk like the last dregs of Power – the Nietzschean ' last men' erased from the Earth and its memory forever. The stuff of science fantasy has become the nightmare of post-historic reality. Leaders no longer exist, nor the servants that connive at their perpetuation. Truly free men have inherited everything, proud ogres answerable only to themselves. Hierarchy will never re-establish itself in the anti-social society of the future. The clock cannot be turned back – there is no clock, not even Big Ben, collapsed in on itself like a detonated Totem-pole. And yet the cycles of eternity have continued revolving, reviving an era of Promethean primitivism combined with the apotheosis of post-modern consciousness.

The Millennium Dome has been flattened into the mephitic gangster-ground it stood upon, its vacuous Disney-Zones for

Disney viewers squashed down like polystyrene cups on a table-top. The Real IRA would have left it like they did the Baltic Exchange, a thread-hanging box of shards. But the Outcast Elect have grown like Gog-Magog and literally crushed it underfoot, hammer-stamped it under Diabolical decree. The Wheel has sunk without trace to the eroded bottom of the Thames, which has flooded far and wide, the once water-tight Barrier submerged in the estuarial swamp. St. Paul's has been reduced to a mere mote in the eye of the Luftwaffe – the atoms that are not the cathedral, as envisaged by Dr. Johnson. A few churches remain, like galleries and museums and labyrinths of the spirit surrounded by barren desert and the graveyard of humanity. Docklands has been gutted and shelved like a metropolis of Lego bricks. The Canary Wharf Tower twinkles no more. Greenwich has been THOUGHT out of existence. The inner and outer suburbs have been buried with the brown sites in the green fields blessed with black. The odd quirky or strange house survives on a seeming-symbolic grid. Everything is deathly dark, save the residual furnace-glow of the charcoal City meeting the red glare in the eyes of its new coveters. What is going to happen now is not a question raised in any head – things are done differently already, no agendas are required. The sky is the only true colour of hopelessness, portending an indescribable Destiny. The Ancient Britons might have recognized this terrain after a freak storm. Their souls are resurrected along with the Giants of Albion.

The Outcast-Elect have come into their element, if not their inheritance as such. The future tense no longer applies to their Diabolical dreams – tenselessness obtains in a manifold Present. The planet is theirs to play with as they please. There is no call to re-write History. History is already UNWRITTEN. History will not be WRITTEN in future. History is to be enacted in a long Moment. There is enough space for the remaining few to create as they choose, without crossing one another's paths – such is the essence of absolute freedom. And only absolute freedom is worth having. Relative freedom was the abiding curse of past civilizations. No Individual wants to compromise his freedom. That is why it is so essential that no inhabited planet should ever become overcrowded. The Outcast may be a Fascist, but only in the interests of preserving his presumed birth-right as a free Being unrestricted by the Burden of a handed down legacy. Mankind made its mistake a long time ago. It deserved to pay for it. The Myth of the Collective destroyed the true spark of Genius that made Man uniquely what he was and is, an unbounded creator of irreducibly Singular realms. Only the Individual, unfettered by the Group-Mind and Identity, can achieve this. Only the Individual exists, for nothing can exist outside the separate consciousness of each Individual. Everything in the Cosmos forms a web spun from the fabric of atomized mind-stuff. And the Great Outcasts of History have always understood this best. That is why they were cast out. Their greatness lay in their REFUSAL to surrender to Society, in their unswerving dedication to the pursuit of their own paths. In that dedication lay the source of their continuing survival and their potential for wresting the mantel of the Superhuman. Only then was their victory assured. No Name Now was a gifted visitation to these fiery Few, a Being from beyond the stars and yet of the very essence of wayward Man.

He still resides in the ruined Architectonic of Human Civilization, a shifting yet seamless entity. Parts of him are now present on other inhabited planets – of which there are many in the Cosmos – wreaking the necessary havoc for the desired emancipation. On Earth he stays sternly solitary in his corporeal aspect, while regulating the elements in his spiritual aspect – the foul breath-source of this doomed Rock. His Brethren occupy their own enlarged domains, holding court like tutelary deities impervious to rivalry in neighbouring domains. The Annihilator has nothing left to destroy, so must merge into the moonscape of his revolutionary madness. Syfert squats like Satan on the throne of Hades, conqueror of cabals and avatar of night through eternal aeons. Obscurius whispers his mephitic mantras in the release of decayed gases. Dr. Plague absorbs the fall-out from nuclear and bio-chemical plants, adding layer on layer of deformity to his gross, reptilian physiognomy. Elethea and Antarctica are dissolved spirits of fire and ice, colouring the Void in sheets of maroon and silver, spiriting the Sphinx from Ozymandian sands to straddle London's ruins. And far away from London on his timeless Estate, Edwin Clore survives with Solarius and Aleph and his animals, silently enacting the Higher Lawlessness in the aftermath of the Meta-Apocalypse. The trio have been unseen by human eye and unheard by human ear since the rupturous exit of their Brethren under the greater spell of No Name Now and Syfert. Utterly abandoned in reclusivity, their self-sufficient solipsism perfectly complements the complete erasure of hierarchical life-forms elsewhere. Communications issue from isolation's deeps.

Humanity has been wiped out everywhere by its rejects and their guardian devils. It will never re-evolve. For now and ever more, the planet is returned to the hideous hands of monsters. Like Minotaurs at the End of the Millennium, growing through the Earth's crust from the boiling lava below, they engulf the world and break free of the solar and lunar orbits – spinning away into the cold and infinite reaches of outer space.

ABOUT THE AUTHOR

Adam Daly was born in 1954 and has spent most of his life in London. In the 1970s he took degrees in Philosophy and the Social Sciences, following all this up with a mandatory Bohemian, unemployed, anti-careerist spell, but has since worked in a variety of occupations, including Sales, for his sins, and more recently as a London Tour-Guide.

The Outcast's Burden is his second book, written in 1999. His other, unpublished books are *The Nameless Revolutionary* in two volumes, and *The Grimoires of Ham'stede*. He has also written a collection of short stories under the title *The Print Psychopath*, extracts from which have been published by *Abraxas*, numerous essays and much poetry.

Aside from Literature and Politics, he lists his main interests under the rousing Rubric of the 'Four Ms' – Metaphysics, Mathematics, Magic and Martial Arts. He is presently researching, somewhat fitfully, a supremely philosophically ambitious work of Science Fantasy, *The Resurrection Men*, which he may never finish, but if so the unfinished product may yet become a treasured curiosity for sinister sleuths a hundred years from now.